# THE ADVENTURES OF AMANDA DARK

RUSS CROSSLEY

53RD STREET PUBLISHING

The Adventures of Amanda Dark

Copyright © 2019 Russ Crossley


Cover art ©Sandralise
Cover designed by R. Edgewood
Cover design and layout © 2019 by 53rd Street Publishing
Print ISBN 978-1-927621-72-1

53rd Street Publishing
Head office: Gibsons B.C. Canada
www.53rdstreetpublishing.com

This is a work of fiction. Any similarities to persons living or dead are purely coincidental.

# ACKNOWLEDGMENTS

Thank you to Rita for being the inspiration for these stories.

# DEDICATION

*For my late mother, Kathleen, who encouraged me to read from an early age. And to all the strong women, like my mother, who have enriched my life.*

# INTRODUCTION

I wrote these Amanda Dark stories originally when I was developing romance characters many years ago. There is a romance angle in these stories, but they are principally paranormal adventures of a woman with the unusual ability to communicate with the spirits of the dead and help them to cross to their final destination. Along the way Amanda must wrestle with her own personal issues and confront her greatest fears.

I hope you enjoy these stories because I am writing a full-length novel involving Amanda — entitled Dark Territory — that will be available in the near future.

Russ Crossley

Gibsons, B.C.

September 2019

# HOOK ISLAND

*This is the origin story of Amanda Dark.*

Amanda held out the flashlight, but the muddy beam of light barely penetrated the inky, thick darkness more than a few feet ahead. Her heart beat loudly in her ears as she carefully stepped forward on the rickety, wooden dock. She glanced over her left shoulder to see Pierre in the launch he'd used to bring her to this isolated island off the coast of South Carolina. She swallowed hard and, for the hundredth time, doubted she'd made the right decision.

"Pierre!" she called. "Which way?"

Squinting into the nearly impenetrable darkness, Amanda could just barely make out Pierre's shape, bathed in the glow from the instruments in the dash of the boat. Pierre had been at first understandably reluctant, but once she'd flashed a hundred-dollar bill, he'd readily agreed to transport her to Hook Island. The transplanted Cajun, originally from New Orleans but who'd moved here following Hurricane Katrina, was amiable and friendly during the ride from Isle of Palms. She sensed that he thought she had a screw loose, but if anyone had told her she would make such a trip in the dead of night, she might have agreed.

"Straight ahead!" She heard his voice echo over the sound of the rhythmic waves ahead of her in the darkness.

Amanda swiveled her head back and forth, still unable to see her way along the dock. Her night vision was terrible—a definite problem for a paranormal investigator who often worked at night. Her breathing was rapid, and her mouth and nose were filled with the smell of wet sand, salt air, and the acidic odor of rotting seaweed. "Too bad I can't lose my sense of smell on command," she mused under her breath.

She carefully moved one foot ahead; the boards creaked. If she didn't walk off the edge of the old dock, no doubt it would collapse beneath her.

She should have come in the daytime, but the letter had said it was a matter of life and death. She had seen enough ghosts to know death intimately, so she had dropped everything back home in Boston and caught the first plane to Charleston. Of course, the certified check for five thousand dollars had certainly added to her motivation to come quickly.

Such a large deposit had surprised her until she'd done some research on the plane using her iPad. According to the websites she'd surfed, her mysterious benefactor, Phillip Swann, was a descendant of the notorious pirate, Captain Henry "Blackblood" Swann who'd sailed these waters in the mid-eighteenth century. Captain Swann had pillaged French, British, and Spanish ships for gold, silver, slaves, coffee, and anything else of value. There were suggestions that once he'd captured a vessel, he would set the crew adrift in lifeboats before setting fire to their ships. This last part of the legend was unconfirmed; but, if true, Swann hadn't been as despicable as many of his contemporaries.

Her immediate problem wasn't proving the truth behind the musty legend, it was surviving the trip from the dock to the Swann family house somewhere on this speck of sand and rock. She'd survived worse, but not being able to see where she was going in pitch blackness had always been her greatest fear.

The beam from her flashlight flickered twice, then went out. Just great, she thought. Now what am I gonna do?

She stuck the tip of her tongue out one side of her mouth and concentrated on her footing. She then took one step and heard a crack as her foot dropped through a hole in the boards. Oh-oh. Not good.

Trying to extract her foot, she lost her balance and stumbled forward. She lost her grip on the small suitcase in her right hand, and it flew away from her to be lost somewhere in the darkness. A twinge of relief came over her when she heard it land on sand. At least her extra blue jeans, shorts, and tops would be dry, and her iPad and cell phone would still function; saltwater destroyed electronic gear thoroughly and quickly. Without her equipment, her trip to Hook Island would be pointless: if there were a ghost, she would need photographic evidence. No photos, no future book; no future book, no food on the table. A girl's gotta eat.

Knowing she was about to fall off the dock, she held out her hands, closed her eyes, and got ready to break the inevitable as best she could; hopefully she wouldn't break anything important. She fell forward and found herself sprawled face-down on sand. Her mouth had filled with the stuff, and she spat out the sticky grains as best she could, but the annoying grit was stubborn and wasn't going without a fight. She'd never liked the beach; there was too much sand, too much wind, and too much saltwater for her liking.

When she tried to lift her head, overwhelming dizziness gripped her, accompanied by a wave of nausea. She set her head back on the sand. The feeling passed, but she realized there was a half-buried stone in the sand sticking up. She must have struck her forehead against it. A growing warmth pooled around her forehead, confirming her theory that she was bleeding. The unmistakable odor of blood flooded her nostrils. Oh, crap. So not good.

She suppressed the urge to cry. I'm going to die on a desert island, in the dark, alone. She investigated the paranormal; she didn't want to become part of it—at least, not yet. I'm too young to die.

The panic gripping her faded, replaced by rationality. I need to stop wallowing in self-pity, she scolded herself. Just because Paul left with the cat doesn't mean I have to fall to pieces during every tiny crisis. Oh-oh ....

As if a window had closed, Amanda's world abruptly disappeared.

~

Amanda's eyes fluttered open, and through fuzzy vision came streaks of filtered sunlight across a wooden ceiling. Her vision cleared and she shifted her head to the left. There was a window, framed by shredded curtains. The glass in the window was missing, so a breeze made the curtains billow like torn rags in the wind.

Shifting her legs, she realized that she lay on her back, her head resting on a severely squashed pillow. The air reeked of dust and mildew. Her mouth was devoid of moisture. She ran her tongue over her dry lips, then gradually rose up on her elbows until she was sitting up. She blinked and her dry eyeballs clicked.

Her head throbbed. Instinctively, she placed one hand on the side of her head, and her fingers brushed a bandage wrapped around her wounded noggin. Now she recalled the fall off the dock. It must have been a while ago since it wasn't night anymore, as evidenced by the sunlight creating a spotlight effect on the dirty wood floor.

She froze when, from a corner of her left eye, she saw movement. Looking down, she saw a black cat with a white-tipped tail padding across the room. Unable to look away, Amanda watched the cat until it vanished into a wall.

Her heart beat a little harder and she sucked in a breath. The cat hadn't been real—at least, not anymore. It was a ghost.

Amanda had seen strange things, but never an actual ghost. Most of the paranormal activity she'd witnessed was minor stuff: objects moving by themselves, sudden fluctuations in room temperature, mysterious breezes on a calm night, and things that go bump in the night. She'd never seen a real, live ghost. Uhhhh ... correction, a real dead ghost.

Amanda let her head sink back to the pillow and closed her eyes. I must be seeing things ....

"Hello—Miss Dark?"

Amanda's eyes popped open. Standing at the side of the bed was a square-jawed man, his chin and cheeks covered in dark stubble. His jet black, curly hair was cut short and his eyes were as blue as a Caribbean sea. His lips formed a wry smile and his eyes twinkled.

"Uhhh ... yeah ...; I'm Amanda Dark." Her brow wrinkled as she eyed the man. "Are you Phillip Swann?"

He nodded. "You really didn't have to come out here in the middle of the night."

She cringed inside. He was correct, of course, but for some reason she'd sensed that he needed her as soon as possible. She had no idea where the sense of urgency had come from, just that it had. "You're right, of course, Mr. Swann."

He chuckled. "Mr. Swann was my father. Please call me Phillip."

His smile disappeared and he arched one eyebrow, sending a shiver of longing through her. She hadn't had a steady boyfriend since high school, when, immediately after the grad party, Dave

Allister had announced he was going back east to college and broken up with her; he'd broken her heart. That was, of course, after they'd had sex ....

Since then, she'd dated occasionally, but nothing had stuck. Of course, after college, she'd become a paranormal investigator. Men didn't seem to like women who chased dead things. When Paul, her only serious boyfriend after Dave, had left, he'd made that much clear.

"Hello, Phillip." She held out her right hand, which he grasped lightly in his as they shook hands. His warm, gentle touch sent shock waves of desire through her unlike anything she'd ever experienced; not even with Dave, in the back seat of his father's Durango, back in her high school days.

"I thought I'd better come as quickly as possible," she explained. "Your letter said it was a matter of life and death."

Phillip's cheeks glowed crimson, his eyes averted; instead of looking at her, he looked in the direction of the window. He moved toward it and gazed out at the rolling surf of the ocean beyond the few trees that stuck up from the tan-colored sand in front of them.

Amanda rose to a seated position and then swung her legs over the side of the bed. Her head throbbed, but she ignored the pain. She came up behind Phillip and detected a sense of sadness emanating from him. For most of her life, she'd had the gift of empathy. She couldn't read thoughts but had a strong sense of feelings.

It certainly made her life interesting at times, and not always for the good. Back in high school, she'd managed to avoid the bullies when she detected their feelings toward her. Of course, it didn't hurt when your best friend, Mary Olson, was captain of the lacrosse team. Mary was as tough as any boy and had been known to flatten a few.

Amanda placed a hand on Phillip's shoulder. He jerked his

shoulder away from her touch as if her skin were on fire. "Sorry," she whispered, dropping her arm to her side. She waited.

He turned to face her. He forced a thin smile on his lips. "I'm sorry; it's just, my wife ...." His voice trailed off and his next words caught in his throat.

"I'm sorry, I didn't know you were married." She sensed his sadness. "Did something happen to her?"

Phillip's watery gaze locked with hers. "No; not really. She lives in Alaska. With my ex-partner."

Amanda wondered if maybe she'd trod on forbidden ground. "Sorry. It's none of my business. I—"

"It's okay, Miss Dark. Your empathy is a gift. Yes—I know about your ability to sense feelings. I wondered if it were true when I hired you. I can see it is; maybe a little too true."

Amanda raised both eyebrows. "What do you mean?"

"My wife left me ten years ago. We were high school sweethearts, but, after our marriage, it became clear our lives were on different paths. I still care about Julie, but we've both moved on."

Testing of her abilities was expected, so Amanda wasn't insulted or annoyed. Honestly, if she were in a client's shoes, she would doubt as well. When you say it out loud, 'a woman who chases ghosts for a living' sounds like rubber room time. "Are you married now?" She winced. "Sorry, that's really none of my business."

Phillip laughed. "No worries. I'm just glad you're here." He arched an eyebrow. "And no, I'm not married. Divorced."

Time to change the subject. "Did you see a cat?"

The sexy smile disappeared from Phillip's features. He frowned. "Cat? Was it black, with a white-tipped tale?" Amanda nodded. "And did it disappear out this window?" He pointed to the window. "Or through a wall?"

Amanda's eyes widened. "How did you know?"

Phillip nodded. "Come with me into the old library."

Amanda followed him out of the bedroom into a wide, musty hallway. They walked side by side to the end of the hall, where there were double doors. The original brass handles were now black with age and lay on the floor where they'd fallen as the doors had rotted away.

Phillip pushed the doors open and they went in. The old library walls were covered in shelves of rotting books; the odor of decay was heavy in the air. At one end of the room sat a large, grandly carved oak desk. On the desk was a hand-carved wooden box, about the size of a modern briefcase—only it clearly wasn't modern. The carvings depicted slaves harvesting tobacco leaves and a sailing vessel with its sails bulging from the wind. There was also a grinning skull over crossed swords, a classic motif for flags of the pirate age.

Amanda concluded that the box had once been the property of one Captain Blackblood Swann, Phillip's ancestor. Her eyes flitted to Phillip, then back to the box. Phillip certainly didn't look like a bloodthirsty pirate, or like any of the ugly pirates in those Disney movies. Actually, he looked more like the pirates adorning the covers of steamy romance novels. A sun-warmed face turned nut-brown, dark curls, and muscular arms clearly visible beneath his denim shirt, the top two buttons of which were undone to reveal a wisp of dark hair. His looks alone stirred her more than any man had in a long time.

Phillip moved to the desk and flipped open the lid of the box to reveal a well-worn, leather-bound book inside. A strong smell of leather filled the room. He gingerly lifted the book from the box and set it flat on the desk. Carefully, as if handling the Dead Sea Scrolls, he turned the yellowed pages to the middle of the thick volume.

Amanda stepped closer to study the odd writing. The words were written in a calligraphic style, the words ornate and flowing. "What is it?" she asked.

"The diary of Captain Henry Swann."

Amanda's eyes widened. "Really? "

He nodded. "The pages are brittle with age, so after we find the treasure, I plan to donate the book to the Smithsonian."

Treasure? A frown creased Amanda's brow. I nearly kill myself, and the life-and-death mission I'm on is to help him find gold and silver? Amanda wasn't rich—in fact she was on the low side of middle-class—but she wasn't a treasure hunter. To her, contact with paranormal phenomena wasn't about seeking lost objects or obscene wealth; it was about helping the dead achieve their just reward or at least be released from earth to go on their way. Sometimes they didn't appreciate her intervention, but the living relatives generally did.

"What's this about treasure?" she said, straining to keep the anger in her gut from her tone.

Phillip swiveled to face her. He offered her a lopsided grin. "Sorry. I'm not a treasure hunter, if that's what you're thinking. No, I'm after something much more personal."

Amanda eyed him quizzically with one eyebrow cocked. Did he have her ability to sense emotions too? "What does his diary say?"

Phillip's shifted back to gaze down at the pages of the open book. "Captain Swann's diary says he had a cat. A black cat with a white-tipped tail. Its name was Scars."

Amanda's eyes went wide, and she stepped to his side, her eyes on the pages. "Really? I saw a cat like that in my room ...." Her cheeks grew warm. "Uhhh, I mean your room... uhhh ... I mean the bedroom." Oh, crap he's gonna think I'm an idiot. All she wanted to do right now was crawl into a dark corner and die of embarrassment.

Phillip, however, didn't seem to notice her sudden discomfort. His eyes were on the pages of the book. "Yes, I expect you saw the ghost of his cat."

Amanda shivered as a sudden coldness enveloped her, accompanied by a feeling of dread. She'd experienced feelings like these before during investigations in haunted houses, but never with this intensity. Her heart beat hard, and time seemed to slow down.

A sharp movement at the edge of her left eye made her turn her head slightly in that direction. What she saw made her freeze and draw in a ragged breath. Her heart beat rapidly. A man dressed in pirate garb, with a long saber dangling from his belt, his dark eyes scowling at her, and his white, frilly shirt stained with dirt, stood eyeing her with one hand resting on the hilt of the sword. His free arm cradled the cat she'd seen earlier, its white-tipped tail flicking to and fro. Could it be a hallucination caused by the blow to the head?

"Uhhh, Phillip, do you see him?"

Phillip looked at her, his eyes quizzical. "Who?"

Amanda pointed to where the pirate with his three-cornered, wide-brimmed hat sporting a black feather, stood silently watching them. Phillip scanned the spot she was pointing to and shook his head.

"I don't see anything ...." His words trailed off and his face became the color of ash. "A ghost," he whispered. His hands were trembling. "You see a ghost, don't you?"

"Yes. At least, I think I do."

"You mean you've never seen one before?"

Amanda swallowed hard as she placed one hand on his arm. She needed to steady herself before she collapsed. Any second, her knees would buckle, and she'd drop to the floor. "As strange as it sounds, no, I've never seen a live one ... uhhh, I mean, a dead one ...." Her mouth clamped shut to stop herself before she shoved both feet into it.

"What's he look like?"

Amanda shifted her gaze to the pirate, who eyed her curiously. He carried the cat to a chair across the room and sat down, now petting the cat with his other hand. The cat curled its tail lazily around its body and looked very content. Its unblinking, mustard yellow eyes watched her.

"Well, he's a pirate and he has a cat. He's sitting on the chair—"

"Sorry to interrupt, Amanda, but there aren't any chairs in here. Haven't been in about two hundred years."

"Actually, he's sitting on one right over there ...." Amanda nodded to the spot where the pirate sat watching her. He wore a half-smile now. Amanda's fear had dissipated, replaced by growing annoyance. He was laughing at her. She was the only one who could see him, and he found her predicament funny. Although, truthfully, she'd find her hard to believe, too.

"Listen, Phillip, if I tell you there's a pirate over there sitting on a chair, then there is. I never lie. I don't know why I see him or his cat, and he may be the first ghost I've seen in the fle—in person, but I am a paranormal investigator. It's my job. It's what I do." She wasn't sure the pirate was real, but she wasn't about to let anyone think badly of her chosen profession. Too many people thought paranormal investigators were scam artists and charlatans—until they needed her services.

Phillip held up his hands in mock surrender. "Okay, okay, I did check you out. I know you're a paranormal investigator, and according to my sources, you're a darned good one."

Amanda took a step away from him and eyed him with a scowl marring her forehead. "You checked me out. With whom?"

Phillip dropped his arms to his sides, rolled his eyes, and emitted a soft chuckle. "Trust me, Amanda, it's nothing untoward, I assure you. I'm a lawyer in Boston, where you also live, and I have a client who used your unique services a couple of years back. Do you remember Ollie Hardson?"

She did indeed remember Ollie, the man she'd dubbed 'the roamer' because his hands often ended up in the wrong places—like on her bottom—at the most inappropriate times. She also recalled helping him remove the ghost of his dead Aunt Grace from his ancestral home. Of course, he'd then sold the old house to a developer for a small fortune. It was a strip mall now.

"You know Ollie?" she said.

Phillip snorted. "Yeah; real creep." He shook his head. "I did the legal work on the sale of the house you cleared of his aunt's ghost. He told me all about it." He chuckled. "Never seen a guy so scared in all my life. His story reminded me of the ghost stories we used to tell around the fire at Camp Wobegon when I was a kid. But if there was one thing about Ollie, it was that he convinced me the tale wasn't fantasy."

Maybe Phillip wasn't such a bad guy—if he was telling the truth. "Why don't you tell me what this is really all about?"

Phillip glanced at the watch on his left wrist. "I imagine you're hungry. Why don't we eat, and I'll tell you all about it? And then if you don't want to help me, fine—you can keep the money and I'll call for a boat to take you back to Isle of Palms, no questions asked. Deal?"

Amanda considered his words. Phillip Swann was growing on her. And he seemed trustworthy—for a lawyer. She nodded. "Deal." Her stomach rumbled. She looked at Phillip, her eyes wide with horror. He laughed first, then she joined in.

Before they left the library, Amanda stole a quick glance at Captain Swann, who was still seated with Scars curled in his lap. He nodded when she walked past him. His expression was pleasant. A pleasant pirate, who woulda thought?

Phillip surprised her when they went out the back door off the kitchen of the old house. The kitchen was beyond repair. Every wooden surface was cracked by wind and heat, and the glass in the window frames here, too, was absent, so there was nothing to keep out the inclement weather when winter storms brushed the island. Phillip explained that the family home had been abandoned just prior to the Civil War. Parts of the house had been damaged when the Confederate army had used the house as a headquarters from which to launch troops or ships against Union forces. In an attempt to drive out the rebel army, the Union navy had bombarded the island just as they had nearby Fort Sumter, but they had never succeeded in dislodging the Confederate troops.

At the rear of the house, Phillip had erected a tent, and, to create his own shaded area, he'd tied the corners of a tarp to the trees ringing his campsite. In the center of the camp was a fire pit, a shallow pit dug in the soft sand and clay, ringed by large, smoke-blackened rocks. A stainless-steel grate covered the pit. Off a tripod over the pit hung a steel hook holding an old-fashioned cast-iron cooking pot.

"Water?" Phillip asked, waving her to a camp chair to the right of the fire pit.

She nodded and sat in the chair. The air was rife with wood smoke. To the right of the tent was a pile of firewood.

He went to an orange cooler and took out two bottles of water, one of which he handed to her before squatting next to the pit and lighting the fire. Soon a blue-and-yellow flame danced under the grate, the wood snapping and popping as the moisture in the wood was heated and expelled. A trail of white smoke disappeared into the sky overhead.

Amanda broke the seal on the bottle and twisted off the cap. After taking a long swig of the cool water, she put the cap back on the bottle and placed it in her lap. "You seem to have been here for a while."

Phillip was concentrating on nursing the growing fire. "Yeah," he said, "a while. I was waiting for you. I sent the letter two weeks ago." He shrugged. "I didn't know how long it would take, so I may have over-prepared."

The fire crackled brightly, and the flames now licked the grate. Satisfied, Phillip rose to his feet and moved to the cooler again. "Hot dogs okay?"

Since tubes of 'mystery meat' were one of her favorite food groups, Amanda readily agreed, but, just as she did at home, she promised herself to eat better in future.

He glanced at her and grinned. "Good. Mustard, ketchup?"

Again, she nodded.

Soon they were eating grilled hot dogs in silence, the smoke from the fire permeating everything.

Amanda swallowed a bite of meat, bun, and mustard-ketchup mixture. She broke the silence first. "What's the treasure that you're so interested in, if it's not gold and jewels?"

Phillip stopped eating and looked at her. His eyes were serious; she worried she might have offended him. "I'm hoping the chest buried somewhere on this island holds the truth about my famous ancestor."

Her curiosity aroused, Amanda continued. "I gather there is a letter or document that will tell a different story about Captain Swann than the tales told in the history books?"

Phillip took a small bite of his hot dog and nodded. "Yes. I believe there is a letter signed by Queen Anne of England affirming that Captain Swann was an agent of the Queen in the Caribbean, raiding Spanish and French colonies and their ships to disrupt trade."

"That's very different from what's recorded about your ancestor." Amanda frowned. "Why is this so important to you now? Surely, after three hundred years, it doesn't really matter all that much, does it?"

Phillip's face became a mask of determination, his jawline taut. He threw the remainder of his meal into the fire. The fatty meat flared, and she could smell it charring. "Before my father died of cancer last year, he made me promise to clear the Swann name." He stopped and looked into her eyes. She watched his eyes lose their hard edge and his shoulders relax. "Sorry. I must seem a little obsessed. I may be, but Dad always felt the reason Captain Swann's name was dishonored involved family land claims in England."

"Land claims?"

"Yes. When Queen Anne died in 1714, King Charles I assumed the throne. He was German and had little interest in English affairs of state; those he left to Sir Robert Walpole. The Walpoles and the Swanns were not on the best of terms since the Walpoles wanted the Swann lands, and because of a love affair that ended badly between cousins from each family."

Sounds like Romeo and Juliet, thought Amanda. She took a bite of her hot dog, chewed, and swallowed. "They didn't like each other. So, what does this all have to do with Queen Anne's letter?"

Phillip shook his head. "Walpole had all copies of the letter destroyed and announced that the English navy would hunt down Captain Swann and hang him as a pirate, which they did in 1719. My grandfather told me something Walpole didn't know was that a single copy of Queen Anne's letter with the royal seal remained hidden on this island. Over the years, we've tried many times to find it without success."

Amanda finished her meal and felt rejuvenated. She took a sip of water, then said, "You want me to ask Captain Swann where the chest is hidden. Correct?"

"Yes."

"And I suppose there are jewels and gold buried with the document."

Phillip smiled. "I don't know. And frankly, I don't care."

"But I do," said a deep male voice to Amanda's left. Looking to the row of trees where the voice came from, she saw a tall, dark-skinned man step out from behind a tree. Her heart froze. In his right hand, he held a snub-nosed pistol pointed at them.

Phillip chuckled. "Ah, yes, Jim Sweet, my former partner. How nice of you to drop by. How long have you been listening?"

The corner of Sweet's mouth curled up. "Long enough to know you may have found the key to finding the treasure." He waved the gun at Amanda. "Her."

Phillip made a move to stand, but Sweet waved the pistol at him. "Don't move," said Sweet, his eyes narrowing.

Phillip's shoulders slumped and he remained seated. "Okay, Jim, you win. What do you want?"

"I want this little lady to accompany me inside the house, talk the ghost into telling me where the treasure is hidden, and then I'll be on my way."

Phillip arched an eyebrow. "What about me?"

"I was thinking I'd dispose of you first, but if the captain won't talk to me, I may still need you. So, I'm going to tie you up and leave you here. If I need you, I'll come back for you. If not ...." Jim left the rest to their imagination, not that it needed much to see that he was going to kill them both, regardless of what happened. As the pirates used to say, dead men tell no tales.

If there was a treasure buried with the letter about Captain Swann, it would be worth a fortune in today's money. People have killed for far less.

"You," Sweet pointed the pistol at Amanda, "find a rope and tie him up."

Amanda looked to Phillip. He nodded and pointed to the tent. "There's a rope inside."

Amanda's thoughts grew cold. They were going along with this man? Why?

Soon, after some instruction by Sweet, she had Phillip tied to the chair.

"Let's go," Sweet said, his voice menacing, his eyes flat with no emotion. How did Phillip get hooked up with such a man, someone capable of killing in cold blood?

Amanda started walking toward the house, followed by Sweet, who had the gun pressed into her back. One thing her father had insisted she learn before she left home to move to the big city was how to use and care for guns. She didn't really like guns, but when someone has one pressed into your spine, knowledge of that sort can come in handy. Six hours a week at a gun range for three months made a girl fairly proficient with firearms.

She entered the house and went immediately to the library, where they'd left the diary open on the weathered desk. Amanda was disappointed to see that the chair, Captain Swann, and his cat were missing.

Moving to the book, she pretended to read it. Her eyes flitted to movement as Sweet came from behind to stand beside her. He had the gun pointing to the floor at his side. He didn't see her as a threat.

A small smile played across Amanda's lips. Once his attention was on the book, she decided her opportunity would never be better, so she reached for the gun and managed to grab it and twist it out of his hand before he could react.

Stepping away, she raised the weapon and pointed it at Sweet's chest. A quick glance confirmed the safety was off.

Sweet regarded her with his dead eyes. "Go ahead," he said, "shoot." He took a step toward her and she instinctively took a step back.

One thing her father hadn't taught her was the killer instinct. Shooting paper targets was very different from shooting a living person. Her fingers gripping the pistol began to sweat. "Don't move," she said.

"I don't think you'll fire," said Sweet, stepping closer. He raised one hand and slowly reached for the gun.

"Don't! I will, you know ...."

Sweet grabbed the barrel of the pistol and pulled it from her slick fingers. Amanda's heart sank. She'd failed them both. They were going to die.

Sweet smiled grimly. "Now, stop this nonsense and talk to the ghost about the treasure." He pointed the gun at her forehead. "Right now." he growled, "Or I will shoot you, and I won't chicken out."

"Sweet!" It was Phillip's voice. He had freed himself. Apparently his boy scout skills of tying and loosing knots had finally paid off. Suddenly Sweet and the pistol were no longer menacing her. At her feet lay the tangled mass of two men locked in combat.

Amanda backed up while watching the struggling men until her body was pressed against the wall. Phillip landed a punch on Sweet's jaw and Sweet's head snapped to the right. Bones crunched, and she could see that Philip's knuckles were bleeding. Sweet grunted from another blow and his head snapped back. He raised the pistol, which miraculously he hadn't let go of when Phillip had tackled him.

Gritting his teeth, Phillip grabbed Sweet's arm and twisted it hard backward, causing the pistol to fly out of his hand. The gun struck the wall behind them with a thud, then rattled to the floor. Amanda considered going for the weapon, but if she tried, the two fighting men might knock her to the floor: the room was too small for her to maneuver around them. They leaped to their feet and circled each other warily. Sweet's eyes kept flicking from Phillip to the gun, then back again. Phillip's attention was focused solely on his opponent.

Sweet's hands formed fists. He rushed forward and swung a fist at Phillip's head. Phillip ducked inside Sweet's intended blow and landed a hard blow to Sweet's solar plexus.

The air rushed from Sweet's lungs; he gasped, clutching his belly as he stumbled backward. Phillip stepped forward and landed a punch hard on Sweet's chin. The man's head snapped around and he collapsed into a heap on the floor, where he lay still, his eyes closed. It was over. Phillip had won.

Phillip moved unsteadily on rubbery legs. His lip was bleeding. His left cheek sported a purple bruise that was already badly swollen. He dragged air into his lungs.

Amanda rushed to him. She wrapped her arms around him, partially to keep him from falling and partially to comfort him. She grasped his shoulders and studied his bloodshot eyes. "Phillip, thank you for saving me."

He gave her a weak smile. "No worries."

"Who is he?" She nodded toward Sweet, lying unconscious on the floor.

"My former law partner," Phillip said.

Amanda's eyes went wide. "He's a lawyer? Would he really have killed us?"

"Oh, yes. Jim Sweet was convicted of murdering his wife and his mother-in-law. And that was for one hundred thousand dollars in insurance money. A priceless treasure proved too much for a greedy creep like him." His eyes drooped at the corners. "I should never have told him about my ancestor, but I thought he was my friend."

Amanda's brow wrinkled. "Shouldn't he be in jail?"

"He must have escaped somehow. We have to contact the authorities." They quickly tied Sweet's hands and feet so he would be unable to move once he regained consciousness.

A cold dread washed over her, sending chills up her spine. Maybe it was emanating from Sweet or Phillip, but she didn't think so. She released Phillip, and he leaned against the wall and watched her as she moved to the desk and opened the diary again. She looked back to the spot where she'd seen the pirate before. Sure enough, there he was—seated, as before, on the chair, with the cat in his lap.

"Hello, lass," he said. There was definitely an English inflection in his voice.

Amanda thought for a second or two that she might faint. Not only had she seen her first ghost, but he'd just spoken to her.

"Uhhh ... hello?"

Phillip frowned. "Who are you talking to?"

"He's here again."

"Oh. Quick, before he leaves, ask him where the treasure is hidden."

Amanda opened her mouth to speak, but the ghost rose from the chair, his hand resting on the hilt of his sword. The cat dropped to all fours, its tail waving back and forth.

"Why should I tell you that?" said the ghost.

"Is something wrong?" asked Phillip.

This go-between conversation could get complicated. She had to discover another way to get these two together. "Captain. I'm wondering if you will show yourself to Phillip." She indicated Phillip with a slight nod of her head.

The ghost scowled. He didn't seem open to the idea.

Perhaps if she shared some information about Phillip, the captain might be more agreeable.

"Captain, I'd like to introduce you to your great-great-great-grandson, Phillip Swann."

The ghost arched one eyebrow. She'd tweaked his interest, but not yet secured his cooperation; time to go for broke. She wondered if ghosts had traces of their human emotions remaining. She hoped so. If not, then this would fall flatter than the soufflé she'd tried to make once in Life Skills class. "Before his father died, he asked Phillip to clear his family name."

The ghost's eyebrows rose together, and his dark eyes narrowed. "What trickery be this, lass? I am charged by the Queen herself to be her agent in these waters!"

"That was three hundred years ago. You were betrayed by Lord Walpole, who branded you as a pirate and had you hung in 1719."

The ghost of Captain Swann ran one hand across his throat. She knew she'd triggered a buried memory, and not a pleasant one. She continued her explanation. "Lord Walpole had all copies of the letter destroyed except the one you hid here on the island. In order to clear your name in the history books, we need that letter."

Captain Swann frowned, then said, "Okay, lass, the boy can see me now."

Amanda's eyes flicked to Phillip. His face was pale and his eyes wide. He could indeed see the pirate captain. She worried it might be too much for him, especially in his weakened condition. As she watched, his features relaxed and his demeanor changed. His face became calm and his eyes reflected determination. "Captain Swann, Sir. I'm your great-great-great-grandson, Phillip—"

The ghost captain interrupted him with a burst of laughter, his features now split by a wide grin. "Weren't ya listening to the lass here, boyo? She told me yor tale of woe. Or should ah say, my tale of woe."

Phillip's eyes flitted to Amanda and his cheeks flushed crimson. "Yes, of course." He smiled weakly at her. "She's a special lady, with special powers."

"Lad, if ya press the palm of yor hand six inches to the right of that corner,"—he gestured to one corner of the room—"where the two walls meet, a hidden panel will open. Inside, you will find the letter from mah Queen." With those words, the captain faded, then disappeared only an empty chair remained. Looking around, Amanda saw that Scars the cat had also disappeared.

"Wow. That was something," said Phillip, expelling the breath he'd been holding in. "Do you still see him?" he asked, looking at Amanda.

She nodded. "Let's see what's hidden in the wall," she suggested.

Phillip moved to the corner and pressed the wall as the ghost had instructed. There was a soft click, then, as if it were on a hinge, a portion of the wall from the floor to the ceiling swung inward. The section was no more than six inches wide—not enough to hide a treasure chest, that much was clear. A flurry of dust accompanied the panel opening. Amanda sneezed when the dust filled her nose.

"Bless you," said Phillip. He reached into the open panel and pulled out a four-foot-long tube-shaped leather case. It had a carrying strap on one side, and the size and shape suggested it might contain a map.

Amanda's heart beat rapidly; she was anxious to see what was inside. Phillip carried the case to the desk. She followed. They stood side by side as he opened the top of the case and peered inside. A smile played across his lips, then became a full-blown grin.

"I see a document inside."

"Is it a map?"

"Yes, tell us, Phil; is there a treasure map in there?"

Amanda froze and shut her eyes tightly. Oh, crap, Sweet's awake. How did he untie the ropes? A soft click told her whoever it was had the pistol. They were right back where they'd started. Doomed.

"Well, well, ya, scurvy dog, do ya think I'd let the likes o' you get the drop on me family?"

A bloodcurdling scream made the hair on the back of her neck stand at attention and sent shivers down her spine. The scream ended abruptly, as if a tap had been turned off. Amanda opened one eye to steal a look at Phillip. He, too, had his eyes shut.

After several seconds of silence that seemed like an eternity,

Amanda decided to take a look. She opened her eyes and turned around.

There was no sign of Sweet, the captain, or his cat. All that remained was the pistol, lying on the floor, resting near the wall where their would-be murderer must have dropped it. She tapped Phillip on his shoulder. He turned around.

"What happened?" he said.

Amanda shook her head slowly. "I have no idea. I've never known ghosts to interact with the living. Unless ...." It couldn't be, but it was the only sane explanation—if you could call the paranormal sane. She set her jaw and explained. "I've read about this, but I've never met anyone who's seen it. And least, anyone who's still alive."

Phillip looked at her in awe, his eyes wide. She continued. "In 1891, a man named Simon Polson, a medium reputed to have been to the other side, reported that when ghosts feel threatened or when they're angered, they can will themselves to touch and interact physically with the real world. Polson said it drained them and, in some cases, destroyed them, but if the ghost were powerful enough, they could even drag the living into the spirit world. The living would not be able to escape and would spend eternity neither living nor dead, in limbo."

Phillip shuddered. "Sounds horrible. Do you think that's what happened to Jim?"

Amanda nodded. "Yes, I think so. But as my mother used to say, he made his bed, he has to lie in it."

She turned to the desk and picked up the map case. "If this is the letter, then we need to take it to a museum to get it authenticated. Old documents will crumble unless they're treated with great care. Do you agree?"

"Yes, but I'm anxious to see the letter."

Amanda grinned. "Me as well, but we have to be patient."

Phillip offered her a lopsided grin, which got her juices flowing again. "Perhaps you and I can work together once we get back to Boston. What do you think?"

Amanda wanted to see him again in the worst way possible. Or was it the best? She smiled to herself. "Well, Mr. Swann, I think we can arrange something, but since you saved my life, I must insist you let me buy you dinner."

"Agreed." He held out his hand; she took it in hers, and shook to seal their agreement. Reluctantly she let go.

"Let's pack up your camp and call for a boat. I'm sure Pierre wouldn't mind coming back for us," she said.

Phillip nodded, then took the leather case from her and walked out of the library into the hall.

A small movement to her left shifted her attention from the doorway toward the wall. Scars appeared from the wall, padded to her, and rubbed his body against her legs, emitting a gentle purring sound. She sighed. Not only did she have a new friend and business partner, but somehow, she had adopted a ghost cat.

Amanda watched Phillip go, and it dawned on her that her life was headed on a new path. She might even have discovered a best friend, and maybe more.

Hopefully much more.

# GRIND MANOR

*Amanda finds herself in the middle of a family feud that may be about to turn deadly.*

Amanda Dark stood on the cracked cement sidewalk in front of the crumbling manor house where the taxi had dropped her with one hand buried in the pocket of her wool coat, shivering in the cool fall air. In the other hand, she held a worn brown leather satchel containing two heavy-duty flashlights, three wax candles, a small case with nail files, a set of variously sized screwdrivers, and a box of wooden matches. Like the girl scouts, she was always prepared.

Golden, crimson, and burnt orange leaves danced in the westerly breeze. As if stirred by some unseen hand, the leaves tumbled across the weathered blacktop of the deserted street in front of her. Ignoring the leaves, her gray-green eyes scanned both directions of the street. The air smelled of fall rot mingled with the lingering odor of charcoal from trash fires in the surrounding neighborhoods.

A shiver travelled through her body. She wished one of those fires were here right now. She wasn't what people describe as lean, but she wasn't fat either, so she wasn't a fan of the cold. She liked to think of herself as a medium-build sun worshiper.

Phil certainly seemed to enjoy snuggling with her on the sofa on cold nights, watching old movies. She shifted her feet back and forth to try and keep her circulation going. There were no cars in sight. Where could he be?

No calls ... then, the cell phone in her coat pocket beeped. Aha.

Taking out the phone, she peered at the small screen and saw Phillip Swann's office phone number. She uttered a soft curse under her breath as she keyed the green answer button, then brought the phone to her right ear.

"Yes, Phil?"

"Uhhh, hi, sweetie. I know you're mad because I'm late, but a client dropped in unexpectedly. I'm so sorry. Please forgive me?"

Amanda smiled to herself. Phil sounded so cute when he begged. And a lawyer's hours were often as bad as a paranormal investigator's; she really couldn't be mad at him. She'd just let him think she was annoyed; it might get her a free dinner. She arched an eyebrow, hoping it might be evident in her voice.

"How long?" She couldn't conceal the amused edge in her tone. A quick glance to the glowing horizon told her sunset was less than ten minutes away, and unless Phil had wings there was no way he'd be here in ten minutes.

"I'll be there in twenty."

"You better," she replied, cutting the connection without a goodbye, hoping by doing so to add to his incentive to hurry. Amanda dropped the phone into the pocket of her coat. Her brow wrinkled. Ever since they'd met on Hook Island, where she'd helped Phillip clear his family name, they'd been seeing each other regularly.

It wasn't exactly a boyfriend-girlfriend relationship by the traditional definition, but they had been spending a lot of time together for two people that weren't dating. Of course, since he'd started getting requests at his law practice, where her unique services were the perfect fit, they'd worked together on a number of cases. It was as if some unseen force had brought them together for some as yet undefined purpose.

A soft mew at her feet made her look down, and, sure enough, Scars was sitting on his haunches, gazing up at her with his black eyes as his black tail tipped with white flicked back and forth. The ghost of the 18th century pirate captain's cat had been her constant companion since returning from Hook Island. She didn't mind, actually. Scars made good company, and he didn't need food or a litter box, so he traveled well; in other words, the perfect pet for someone who didn't want a pet. Of course, being a ghost cat that could pass through solid objects made him handy to scout out an old house or tomb for her.

She chuckled to herself. Scars had been her ghost scout cat ever since he'd decided to adopt her—just like living cats, ghost cats adopted you, not the other way around.

Phil couldn't see Scars; only she could. This new ability of hers (with Scars' help) to survey a house or tomb before they entered seemed to impress him even more. He'd already known about her empathic abilities, another handy feature for someone in her profession.

She'd dismissed the idea of her and Phil being more than friends. They enjoyed each other's company, a few snuggles and a few kisses, but that's all. And they were both unattached, so how did a little harmless flirting between consenting adults hurt anyone? She certainly didn't have any plans to sleep with him, though he did stir her juices like no one had before.

Clearing her thoughts of such things, she turned her attention to the long-abandoned manor house beyond the steel fence guarding the perimeter of the yard. Ancient, gnarled-and-knotted-trees dotted the property, reminding her of arthritic old men twisted by time and age. The once lush gardens were overgrown by weeds and choked by vines. The lengthening shadows gave the vines the appearance of invading snakes, twisting and grasping the remaining bushes and trees as if choking the life from them. An occasional bird call cut through the swoosh of the strengthening breeze.

It was a decidedly creepy old house, sitting in the middle of a neglected property. The brick-framed house rose three stories. The rows of windows facing the street on each floor were dark, their brick facade tinged green by moss. The house had a sagging wraparound porch and an ornately carved front door with a massive door knocker shaped like a dragon with its mouth open, as if spitting fire.

From her research, Amanda had learned that the house had been abandoned in the 1960s after the death of the family's only daughter, sister to the twin brothers. One brother had hired Phil's law firm to represent him in an estate dispute with the other twin. These were all the children of the recently deceased, Lord and Lady Grind, who had fled to America after an insurrection in the African nation where they'd lived for over twenty years. The couple's lives had ended in a private plane mishap outside Paris, two years ago.

According to SPOOKRUMORMILL.COM these days, Grind Manor had one lone occupant, a ghost; specifically, the ghost of the sister. Her name was Priscilla. She had died of pneumonia at the age of twenty-three.

Bertram Grind had hired Phil to find a copy of another will, hidden somewhere in this house. He'd claimed the house was haunted, and that when he'd tried to enter on his own, the ghost had chased him off. He'd been too afraid to enter ever since.

Phil had contracted Amanda to clear the house of the dead sister's spirit so that Bertram could search the house to find the wayward will. While it wasn't really her business, Amanda suspected that the will in question differed from the one the other twin, Maxwell Grind, had presented to a probate judge, which bequeathed to him a substantial portion of his parents', the Lord and Lady Grind's, very affluent estate holdings.

According to newspaper reports, Bertram hadn't been cut out completely, but the amount reported was nowhere near the inheritance of his twin brother. Phil had only told her that Bertram disagreed with this assessment of his situation.

I may be just the paranormal investigator, but I can read between the lines like anyone else. Bertram's slice of the old family pie must be miniscule compared to his brother's. In fact, she suspected that the difference was to be measured by how many zeroes there were behind the words 'many, many millions'.

Her thoughts were interrupted when a taxi pulled up to the curb and stopped. Phil shot out of the back seat, stepping onto the sidewalk, and waved to her, his handsome features split by a wide smile. Every time they met, he seemed as pleased to see her as if they hadn't seen each other for a long time.

"Hi," she called. Her cheeks were warm even in the cool breeze; Phillip always made her heart rate rise and her breath come harder. One day, she would act on this, but today was not the day. There was work to be done, first.

The trees surrounding the old house had begun to stir, swaying in the rising force of the wind. The branches brushed each other like the ancient arms of old men. Amanda shivered and pulled up the wool collar of her coat, holding it tighter around her neck. She hoped it wouldn't snow this early in the fall, or getting another cab to come to this end of Boston would be an almost impossible challenge.

Phil moved to the curb side of the cab and leaned in the window of the passenger side, handing the driver a few bills. "Keep the change," she heard him say.

She didn't hear the driver's reply, but the light on the roof of the car lit up and he sped away. She watched the yellow and black car until it disappeared around a corner at the end of the block.

"Whew. It's cold out here," said Phillip, who joined her with his hands buried in the pockets of his ankle-length leather overcoat. "Why didn't you wait inside?"

"I like to survey the outside before I enter a haunted house," Amanda explained. "Besides, I didn't want the client to think I'd walk off with the will if I tripped over it by accident."

He eyed her up and down. "What's with the runners?"

"In case I need to make a fast getaway."

Phil smiled. "OK. Let's go inside. It's wayyyy too cold out here." He approached the steel gate and pulled it open with one gloved hand. The hinges shrieked, but the heavily rusted gate swung aside surprisingly easy. The orange crust covering the steel shattered and rained down on the path like rusty snow.

Ever the gentleman, Phil entered first, then held the gate open for Amanda. She cast a shy smile as she walked past him. His eyes sparkled at her in the gathering dusk as she went by. Her eyes drifted from his to the windows on the second floor—a flash of white light made her stop. She peered at the windows. The light didn't reappear. As expected, they'd already attracted some spectral attention.

Her brow wrinkled, and she arched an eyebrow. The house had been abandoned for decades; she doubted the electricity had been left on. "I think I saw our ghost," she said.

"Really? Where?" Amanda pointed to the darkened windows on the second floor. "I don't see anything," said Phil.

"I saw a light in one of those windows." She locked eyes with Phil. "I don't think the electricity's on, do you?" He shook his head. "Let's go." After she'd approached the wraparound front porch, she stopped to open the satchel. She took out the two flashlights, and, handing one to Phil, clicked hers on. The brilliant white light cut through the growing darkness, illuminating the front porch. At the edge of the beam, Amanda spotted movement and brief flashes of small yellow eyes. This was immediately followed by the furious sound of tiny toenails scratching the boards as rodents clambered over each other to escape the sudden intrusion.

None of this surprised her. Many an old house's occupants were of the vermin variety once the humans vacated—at least the living humans. It often occurred to her that there had to be reasons why the rats and mice weren't afraid of ghosts and ghouls. Do they know something we don't?

Amanda stopped as she tested the boards on the first of three short steps leading from the weed-infested footpath to the porch; they seemed solid enough. "One at a time, Phil. Just in case," she added, nodding at the gray, weathered wooden planks underfoot. He nodded.

Turning away, she carefully walked up the three steps until she stood on the porch. The boards creaked but appeared strong enough to hold her weight—their combined weight might be another matter. She raised one hand to signal to Phil to wait. Just as she did, she froze, her empathic ability detecting something— something that bothered her. At the edge of Amanda's awareness, she sensed a distinct feeling of grief; a surge of sorrow so deep it shook her to the core of her being.

Something bad, something very bad, had happened here. She sensed pure anger from the ghost. It seemed to be an all-consuming anger, and in her experience, this wasn't a good state for a spirit. She didn't sense any evil presence behind it, just a deep sadness leading to frustration. No wonder Bertram had fled the house in a panic. Without an experience with ghosts such as hers, such feelings could be very frightening.

She started walking again until she stood at the front door. The finish on the door was peeling, but still appeared solid. The dragon-shaped knocker was made of solid brass, with an oval loop of brass affixed to the knocker just below the dragon's head. The brass was severely tarnished from the weather; not surprisingly, given it had been there since Grind Manor was constructed in 1947.

Amanda thought about using the ornate door knocker but dismissed the idea as silly. Only the dead were home, and, from what she'd sensed, they weren't going to be all that welcoming to the living.

She hesitated. This was the first time since she and Phil had joined forces that she'd felt failure would have such a high price. Why? Something nagged at the back of her mind; a darkness. It was as if her empathic ability were warning her. She shook off the feeling. In her job, she'd seen a lot of scary stuff; why would this job be any different? But she was having difficulty shaking off her growing sense of unease.

Gripping the brass door knob, she turned it and discovered that the door was unlocked. Glancing over her left shoulder, she nodded to Phil who still stood on the steps, waiting to walk forward. She didn't want him to break an ankle if the boards on the deck gave way. She heard a click as the door latch disengaged, then used the flat of her other hand to push the door in. It swung on rusty hinges, creaking in the silence. It occurred to her that the birds making crying noises from the ancient trees on the overgrown property had gone quiet since she'd entered through the gate. Weird might be her business, but this was too weird.

Scars skittered by her legs as he disappeared into the interior. She wasn't concerned about him. After all, he was dead already, so what was the worst that could happen to him?

Peering through the murky air at the interior beyond the door, she saw the dust floating in the still air, which supported the claim that the house had been abandoned for a long time. Streams of waning sunlight cut through the murky windows, splashing spotlights of light across the dirty tiled entry in the foyer. In the shadows, she could make out a small table set against the short wall at the base of the staircase. On the table rested a half-moon-shaped lamp with a dusty cloth shade covering the light fixture. Cobwebs were draped across every surface and hung off the curved banister guarding the wide staircase that swept upward to disappear into the darkness.

Amanda stepped inside and waved for Phil to follow. She noticed that he'd donned leather gloves. Was he concerned about leaving fingerprints, or touching something icky? Probably both, she mused. She wished now she'd remembered to bring hers.

After pulling out the other flashlight, she flicked the switch on the casing and the powerful halogen light came on, easily chasing the darkness away. Using the beam as her guide, she scanned the foyer and saw two French-made rosewood chairs coated in thick gray dust, one each on either side of the table where the lamp sat.

She swept away the cobwebs that hung like a curtain from the ceiling with the satchel as she moved farther into the room. The heavy scent of must and mold filled her nose and mouth. Suddenly, Scars appeared, running toward her from her left, his glowing emerald eyes reflecting the beam of light from the flashlight. She was glad for Phil's inability to see the cat; if he could have, he'd probably have been freaked out. Scars ran everywhere he went, so his abrupt and hurried reappearance didn't startle her in the least.

Scanning her surroundings, she saw three sets of twin oak doors exiting off the foyer, one each to left and right and one at the bottom of the staircase. She picked the one at bottom of the staircase to investigate first. She set the satchel on the table beside the lamp. She had considered going upstairs to find the room with the window facing the front of the house where she'd spotted the glow, but decided she'd first better see if they could find the library or study. They were here to find a will, and that seemed the most likely location. The ghost could wait, for now.

"Let's find the library," said Phil from behind her, echoing her thoughts.

She grinned to herself. They were so often in sync it scared her.

She moved to the doors she'd selected and turned the brass doorknob. She swung the door open and shone the light inside. Through the floating dust, she saw the room was indeed the library. A thick Persian rug covered the floor; the gold, royal blue, and crimson pattern had a thick coat of dust obscuring its once ornate pattern. An oak desk the size of small car sat to one side of a floor-to-ceiling stone fireplace. Amanda stepped inside, batting at the cobwebs with her free hand. Phil came in after her, closing the door on its squeaky hinges.

"Do you think there's a safe somewhere?" Amanda asked, her eyes focused on the framed painting on the wall behind the desk. Two walls contained floor-to-ceiling bookshelves.

"Yeah. For sure," breathed Phil, his voice low. "This place is really something."

"It sure is, Phil; but where would the safe be?" A faint odor of whiskey and stale cigar smoke lingered in the air. To her, this signaled that the room had been used frequently in the past for after-dinner business, back in the day.

"Uhhh ... I suggest the painting?" Phil swung the beam of his flashlight over the painting. The subject was a sallow-cheeked man with a gray beard and dark, serious eyes. He was dressed in 18th century clothing of a type she'd seen in many of these old houses, and the tangled mass of his hair was comprised of black and gray strands. A metal plate affixed at the bottom edge of the wood frame read Lord Grind, 1744–1799.

Phil moved behind the desk and ran his fingers along the frame's edge. His brow wrinkled, and he next pulled the frame away from the wall with the fingers of his free hand. The painting wasn't hinged like in the movies. He directed his flashlight behind the painting, then pulled it away from the wall as he looked behind it.

After a second or two, he released the painting. It thumped against the wall. "No safe," he said simply.

He ran his flashlight around the room, scanning the books on the shelves. Amanda directed her beam to the floor and studied the carpet. She didn't know what, exactly, she was looking for, but when Scars appeared through the carpet, she knew where the safe was hidden. He wagged his tail at her and mewed softly. She smiled to herself. "I found it."

"Really? Where?"

Directing her beam at the carpet where Scars had appeared, she said, "Under the carpet in the floor."

It took them forty minutes to move two heavy oak side tables, an ottoman, and two leather wing chairs against one of the book cases so they could lift the carpet away in order to access the trap door in the floor. The carpet was surprisingly heavy, but between them, with sufficient sweat, grunting, and groaning, they managed to lift up one corner and fold it back so it was out of the way. It formed a mountain of heavy, thick carpet to one side of the desk.

After they'd caught their breath, Amanda trained her flashlight on the trap door and saw that it had a key lock. Now, where was the key? She arched an eyebrow at Phil. He rolled his eyes and grunted. "Why is it never easy?" he asked, voicing what she was thinking.

"I'll look in the desk drawers," she said. "You check the books for a hollowed-out one."

"Really? Sounds a little Hollywood-ish to me."

She grinned. "Who do you think movie folk consult when they need the spooky details about those old houses?"

Phil chuckled. "Oh? My girlfriend knows Steven Spielberg, eh?"

Amanda stiffened. Phil had used the 'G word', but now was not the time to discuss this. "Just look for the key, smart guy."

He offered her a lopsided grin and his eyes sparkled. Before she could react, he looked away and walked to one of the two book cases. She kept her eyes locked on his back as he began running the palm of one gloved hand over the books. Shaking off the effect his words had caused, she let out the breath she'd been holding in. She started clambering over the carpet until she was behind the large desk.

In the middle was a large single drawer, which she tried first, but as she'd expected, it was locked too. Things were not exactly going to be easy. Then again, too often she was forced to take the harder road.

Grunting from the exertion, she struggled back over the thick mountain of folded Persian carpet and checked with Phil to see if he'd found any keys. He hadn't, so she went the foyer to retrieve her satchel from where she'd left it on the table. Walking back into the library, she sighed as her eyes fell over Mount Persian.

Gritting her teeth, she once again climbed over the carpet until she was behind the desk. Setting the satchel on the desk, she opened it and took out two nail files. One was larger than the other, but as she didn't know which would work better, she decided to try both. Picking up the shorter of the two from where she'd placed them side-by-side on the desk, she stuck the tip in the desk's lock and twisted. The tip broke off in the lock.

Amanda fought the urge to throw the broken nail file across the room. She took in a deep breath, then let it out slowly.

She stiffened when a cold breeze suddenly washed over her. The hair on the back of her neck rose. "Miss Dark?" said a breathy voice. A woman's voice, by the timber.

"Yes …," she whispered.

"Open the bottom drawer on the left," instructed the voice.

Amanda licked her dry lips and opened the drawer as instructed. "What next?"

"Pull the middle drawer toward you." Amanda hesitated. "It'll open. I saw my father open this drawer many times."

Amanda assumed the voice had to belong to Priscilla Grind, the ghost of Grind Manor. She wrapped her fingers around the edge of the drawer and pulled, and sure enough, it slid open, far more easily than she thought it would, considering how long it had probably been closed. The lock had obviously been a ruse to fool would-be robbers or curious people like her.

The pencil tray in the drawer had a few paperclips, two pencils, a pen, and a large steel key. She smiled to herself. "Thank you, Priscilla," she murmured.

"You're welcome, Amanda."

Amanda's cheeks grew cold as the blood drained from her face: she was having a conversation with a ghost. After she meets Phil, she starts to see ghosts; now, she's having full-blown conversations with them. What's next, tea and cookies with the spirits? Maybe her meeting Phil wasn't an accident after all?

Picking up the key to study it, she decided it was about the right size for the trap door lock. She stuck it in the pocket of her black slacks then made her way back over the Persian hill while carrying the satchel. She checked off the first item on her mental mission list as completed. She was confident that the copy of the will would be in the safe beneath that trap door. At least, she hoped there would be a safe. All that was left now was to clear the house of Priscilla and help her on her way to her next destination.

She found Phil, his suit jacket thrown across one of the wing chairs they had moved earlier, standing on a step ladder, testing the books on the higher shelves. "Phil, I have the key," she announced triumphantly.

Phil glanced over his shoulder at her. His face was pale and drawn, she suspected from frustration and weariness. His broad shoulders slumped, and he nodded. He stepped off the ladder and joined her, gazing down at the trap door. She squatted and stuck the key in the lock. The key turned, and there was an audible click. She glanced at Phil and grinned. He nodded, his eyes sparkling with excitement.

The trap door had a steel handle resting in a perfectly shaped hollow imbedded in the steel so it lay flush with the edge and wouldn't protrude. Amanda pulled the handle out and up. The door didn't budge.

Phil dropped beside her. "Let me try," he offered.

Amanda let go of the handle and Phil grabbed it. He pulled hard but again it didn't budge. Would this day never end?

Phil's brow wrinkled. After rolling up the sleeves of his powder blue dress shirt, he gritted his teeth then grabbed the handle with both hands. His cheeks puffed out, and she watched him count silently to three; then he began to pull hard, the muscles in his strong arms straining. His face became red as pomegranate and his arms trembled. He kept pulling until finally, with a loud cracking sound, the trap door flew open, sending him off balance backward.

"Hey!" He landed hard on his tail bone, the air rushing from his lungs. He lay gasping, trying to draw a breath. Dust flew in the air around him, the musty smell stronger than ever.

"What you seek isn't beneath the trap door," said the woman's voice.

Amanda looked around, using her flashlight to scan the library. They were alone. But the voice had been right before. Weird that she didn't see Priscilla. Ever since Hook Island, Amanda had gained the ability not only to sense emotion, but she'd been able to see the ghosts. The feeling of confidence she felt emanating from this unseen spirit was strong and clear, but was it really Priscilla, or some deceptive poltergeist playing the nasty games they were known for? She had been fooled a few times before, not that she wanted to dwell on those dark events.

"So where is it?" she said, mentally crossing her fingers.

"Pull out the middle drawer of the desk; underneath you'll find an envelope taped to it."

Amanda sighed. Back over the mountain once again. "It's not in there," Amanda said. Her voice sounded heavy and dulled by a lack of energy. Closing her eyes, she sagged back on her haunches, overwhelmed by the feeling of total defeat.

"Where?" said Phil simply.

"Taped under the middle drawer of the desk." She nodded her head toward the mountain of carpet. "I can't go over there again ...." Her voice trailed off. Amanda stiffened as fingers brushed her left shoulder. Phil's touch sent shockwaves of passion through her. You pick the worst times, girl.

A calmness came over her. "I'll do it," she heard Phil say. She wanted to open her eyes and watch him, but she didn't want the feeling he'd planted in her to end. Instead, she followed him by the sound of his shoes and the sigh of the carpet compressing under his weight as he clambered over it, and finally, the sound of the drawer being opened, then silence.

"I got it!"

Her heart beat faster. "He loves you," said the voice of the woman.

"Priscilla?" Silence. No response.

She heard the scuff of Phil's shoes as he returned over the pile of carpet. She shot to her feet as her eyes flew open. Phil walked up to stand in front of her. His dirt-smudged face was split by a wide grin. In his right hand he held a manila envelope.

Before speaking, Amanda threw her arms around Phil's neck and shoulders and dragged him into a passionate kiss. She held him for several seconds and sensed no resistance from him. Good; he felt the same way about her as she did about him.

Finally, she released him and they parted. "What was that all about?" he said. "Not that I'm complaining."

Amanda chuckled. "I'll explain later. Show me what you found."

Phil held up the envelope and opened the flap on one end and drew out two documents. "Bertram was right; there was another will. But he neglected to mention his sister had a child. A girl, born in 1967. The parents' names are interesting." he handed her the birth certificate first.

Amanda's eyes went wide when she saw that the baby had the same last name as both her father and her mother. Priscilla was the mother ... while her brother Maxwell was listed as the father. Creepy.

Phil next handed her the will he'd found with the birth certificate, and the baby listed as Melanie Grind was an equal beneficiary in the Grind family estate.

"So, where is this Melanie Grind?"

"I don't know, but I intend to find her. This revelation will probably invalidate the new will arranged by Maxwell. He can't cut out an heir to the estate. Ultimately, a judge will determine who gets what. I suspect this was what Bertram was after all along."

He took the documents from her and stuffed them back in the envelope. After retrieving his suit jacket, he placed his flashlight in the satchel then picked it up and touched her elbow to lead her out of the library. Amanda used her flashlight to light their way.

When they were in the foyer and about to go out the front door, he suddenly stopped. "What about Priscilla?" he asked.

"Don't worry about her, Phil, I'm sure she's fine." In fact, during her review of the documents, she'd sensed that Priscilla had exited this world for good now that she knew her child would receive her rightful inheritance. She'd found her peace at last.

The truth did indeed set you free.

She sensed that not only had this investigation been success-ful, but that her and Phil's relationship was about to take on a new dynamic. Amanda Dark has a boyfriend. I like the sound of that. Something soft brushed her leg. Looking down, she saw that Scars had joined them. His glowing eyes looked up at her as he purred. Her ghost cat appeared to concur with her view.

The adventure in Grind Manor would indeed be a memorable one.

## MOONRISE DINER

*This is a longer story format for Amanda. The stakes in this story are deeply personal for her and will reveal more of her family history.*

The cushions of Phillip Swann's black leather executive chair sighed, breaking the silence of the teak wood-paneled office as he sank into the chair. Amanda Dark sat in a horseshoe-shaped chair, studying him from the other side of his massive glass-topped desk. His intense blue eyes were fixed on the letter he'd unfolded seconds ago after extracting it from the yellowing envelope Amanda had handed him when she'd sat down.

His jet-black curly hair, cut short as usual, appealed to her more every day they spent together. Her heart beat a little faster each time they met. If only he shared her deeper feelings.

The law offices of Smythe, Wellington, Goldberg, and Thompson smelled of wood polish, which wasn't surprising since the Boston law firm had never removed the original teak paneling from the walls since the firm had first opened in 1902. Such expensive wood required constant care to maintain its gleaming, pristine appearance.

Amanda imagined such attention to detail gave the firm's wealthy clients considerable confidence in the expertise of the firm's seventy-five lawyers. Amanda eyed Phillip's square jaw, dimpled smile, and broad shoulders, causing her heart to flutter.

I certainly have confidence in the man I've loved since we met on Hook Island.

Their first meeting had been eventful and dangerous, so it wasn't a stretch to remember those events. Phillip had invited her to Hook Island, hoping she'd use her gift to help the ghost of the notorious pirate, Captain Henry Swann, his ancestor, cross over to his final destination in order to free the him from his wanderings between this world and the next. And to ask Phillip's ancestor for the location of a map so he could find Captain Swann's buried treasure, reported to be worth a fortune.

Since then, Phillip, an estate attorney, had teamed up with her in her role as a paranormal investigator to help a number of tortured souls cross over. The jobs had been rewarding and lucrative for them both. Wealthy clients paid considerable sums for their services.

Phillip finished reading the three-page letter, then set it carefully on his desk. The document was quite old since it dated back to the nineteen fifties. She knew this because it originated in her late father's files.

Amanda had found the envelope in a file folder stuffed with power company bills dated to the early fifties which she'd been about to throw away. She hadn't opened the envelope addressed to her father because the return address was for her Uncle Gib's place in Arizona.

Uncle Gib, her father's older brother, had sexually abused her when she was twelve, so anything he touched repulsed her. Her first thought had been to burn the envelope to a pile of ash for it to join her uncle who no doubt burned in hell, but something deep within her had told her not to destroy this envelope. These feelings were something more than mere emotions; it was important that she listen to the spiritual voices calling to her.

The postmark showed the letter had been mailed from Moonrise, Arizona. The date stamp in the postmark had intrigued her the most because it was the day her uncle had murdered his first wife, Lucy. Or at least, the day he had allegedly stabbed her to death ....

Gib had been acquitted of the murder but had lived under a cloud of suspicion for the rest of his life. Family legend said that Gib had remarried, his second wife also named Luci, like his first wife (the only difference being her name ending in an i instead of a y), who had worked with him as a waitress at the Moonrise Diner. There could have been physical differences as well, but Amanda had never met either of them, so she had no idea what they'd looked like.

As far as she knew, no one in the family had ever met Luci-the-second even after Gib had died. Frankly, Amanda thought there never had been a second wife.

Amanda had searched the on-line newspaper archives after she'd found the envelope and discovered coverage of Gib's trial. There was no mention in any of the news articles referring to a letter mailed to her father on the day of Gib's arrest. And there was no mention of her father having testified at her uncle's trial.

Her father had told her he'd turned his back on his brother after his arrest until after she was born, when they'd reconciled. Her father had never explained how they'd buried the figurative hatchet to settle their differences.

At the time Uncle Gib had abused her she'd feared that if she told her father, it would create another split between the two brothers, so she remained silent. Fortunately, the abuse had only happened once, following which Gib had left Boston for the last time. When Amanda was thirteen, Gib had ended his own life.

She'd blocked his name from her mind for the past fourteen years, until she'd found the envelope.

Phillip, his eyes on the desk, his head forward, didn't say anything for several minutes. The suspense formed a knot of tension in Amanda's stomach and she grew increasingly restless as each second passed; she passed the time by shifting her bottom on the leather chair repeatedly as if unable to get comfortable. Finally, she couldn't contain herself any further. "Phillip, for goodness sake! What does it say?"

Phillip looked up from the desk, his eyes free of emotion, to lock eyes with her. One eyebrow arched on his tanned forehead. "Your uncle wasn't who he said he was."

Her heart skipped a beat. Breathe, girl .... "What do you mean?"

Phillip sat back and sighed. "He claims he was an undercover operative for the Arizona State Police. He says someone killed his wife to send him a message."

"Does he say who?" Now she was extremely interested. This had quickly become a mystery. She loved a mystery.

Phillip gazed at her, a pained expression on his face. "Something about inappropriate advances on a woman." He looked away avoiding her stare.

Amanda's guts twisted, pushing the bitter taste of bile into the back of her throat. She thought she might vomit any second. She shuddered as the awful memory swept over her of her uncle's hands groping her. Memories of the stale liquor on his breath mingling with the smell of salty sweat and the spent cooking grease leaching from his pores paralyzed her.

"Does he know who killed his wife?" she whispered in a trembling voice. Calling on inner reserves, she pushed through the decades of pain and humiliation. Phillip shook his head.

Her Uncle Gib had been a creepy, lying, sack of ..., but he was her beloved father's brother whose wife had apparently been murdered by persons unknown. And who knew now if his death was a suicide? Everything about the letter cast uncertainty on her uncle's life, requiring closer scrutiny. Although, given her history with her uncle, she didn't want to, she resolved to solve this mystery out of respect for her late father.

"I'll call the Arizona State Police, then," she decided. "They'll look into the murder." Phillip shook his head again, the difference this time being that his eyes drooped at the corners.

A sudden burst of anger welled up from deep within Amanda's belly. I don't need his pity.

"Did I say something wrong?" asked Phillip, his eyes wide with concern.

"Why do you ask?"

Phillip's expression relaxed. "Ummm, I know this is a stressful situation, Amanda, and I'm sorry; I truly am." A gentle smile passed over his handsome features.

When she'd brought him the envelope, she'd told him how she didn't like her uncle and that he'd been estranged from the family, but hadn't shared the details of the sexual abuse. But her would-be boyfriend was a smart man; he knew something was very wrong even if he didn't know the details. "But the Arizona State cops are unlikely to take any interest in reopening the case. They seemed convinced your uncle committed the crime."

Amanda picked up the glass of water Phillip had poured for her when she'd first arrived and took a sip of the cool water as the tension in her body eased. "Why not? I'm sure they'll want to catch the real murderer."

Phillip nodded. "Of course; but the case was likely closed after your uncle's trial because they probably still think he was guilty, or got off on some technicality, or had a clever lawyer." His mouth formed a sly smile. "They don't much care for the practitioners of my profession. And if you tell them you're a paranormal investigator, they'll laughed us both out of the police station."

Amanda's cheeks grew warm. "What's wrong with my job?"

Phillip arched one eyebrow. "Now, Amanda, I don't mean to offend you—I know from personal experience you have a special gift, but police officers are born skeptics. They'll never take you seriously." He sighed, then lifted his coffee mug to his lips and took a sip. After swallowing, he added, "I think the better approach is to search the scene of the crime for ourselves. Maybe we'll find something, or someone, that'll help us uncover the truth. Something the cops overlooked all those years ago."

The anger disappeared as Amanda considered his words. He was right. They both knew the something or someone Phillip referred to involved ghosts and the paranormal.

"OK," she said. "The place to start is the town of Moonrise, Arizona. That's where Gib had his diner—his wife, Lucy, died in the diner ...." Her brow wrinkled. "And I seem to recall dad telling me Gib committed suicide in the diner."

Her well-tuned sixth sense told her they would find a horrible truth at the Moonrise Diner—a frightening truth to make her blood run cold.

THE TWO LANES of cracked asphalt making up the main street of Moonrise Arizona were off the state highway on an old bypass carved from the dry, desolate landscape surrounding the abandoned mining town. According to the GPS navigator, the bypass ended five miles north of the town.

Amanda had spent the several hours driving to Moonrise from the Phoenix airport on her iPad reviewing her uncle's trial transcript, which Phillip had managed to obtain for her. She'd been surprised the file even existed any more, but pleased it was available in the Arizona State Government Library.

The transcript did yield some interesting facts. In 1972, Uncle Gib had testified that he and Lucy had had a fierce argument the night Lucy was killed, after which he'd gone to a nearby bar to cool off, ending with him going on a drinking binge. There was a plethora of names related to the case—small time gangsters mostly, with colorful names like Pete "Split Nose" Rostovitch, Jimmy "Beer Belly" Lucia, Al "Stinky" Garbone, and "Maximum Guts" Max Schiller.

Uncle Gib had claimed that one of these gangsters had killed his wife, but his reasons for thinking this were absent from the record. The cops or the district attorney obviously hadn't believed his allegations, or they hadn't wanted to believe him.

She put her iPad away in her handbag as Phillip stopped their rented Jeep in front of the Moonrise Hotel. Amanda expected to see a hitching post for horses and cowboys with ten-gallon hats and leather gun belts strapped to their hips standing on the porch.

Instead, a gray-haired man sat in a rocking chair, reading a newspaper on the porch to one side of the twin doors of the hotel entrance. The doors had glass windows built into the wood frame, allowing her to see the lobby and the front desk. A gray-haired woman stood behind the desk, her eyes focused on something in front of her.

Phillip shut off the engine, then swung the driver's door open as the rumble of the engine died away to be replaced by the soft whisper of the desert wind.

The oppressive heat struck her in the face as soon as she swung her door open. Her skin immediately became damp with sweat as she stepped into the thick, hot air.

Phillip retrieved their suitcases from the back of the jeep, then joined her, walking up the three steps to the wide gray wood porch, the boards creaking underfoot.

The man in the rocker dropped his newspaper and his coffee-colored eyes narrowed. "Heya, you folks lookin' for a room?" His voice had a scratchy quality, like an old phonograph record.

"Yes," said Amanda with a nice-to-meet-you smile on her lips. "We're in town on holiday."

The man chuckled gruffly, letting the newspaper fall into his lap. "Holiday? In Moonrise? That's a good one, young lady." He arched one white eyebrow. "No one holidays in this town. It's nearly dead. Me and the wife are the last of the few who stayed after the silver mine closed."

"When was that?" asked Phillip.

The old man snorted. "Back in '99. The mining company ran out of money ...; they left town along with most of the folks 'round here." He peered into the distance, ignoring them. "We had a pretty young school marm, a church, general store, and even one of them fancy haberdasheries .... Those were the days ...." He scowled, then abruptly raised the newspaper, creating a wall of newsprint between them. "Never been the same since," he muttered.

Amanda shook her head, then caught herself when she spotted the date at the top of the paper in the old man's hands. November twenty-first, nineteen ten.

*That can't be right—has to be a misprint.*

Phillip opened one of the twin glass and wood doors and ushered her inside. Once in the hotel lobby, the smell of dust and sand disappeared, to be replaced by the scent of jasmine, and, though the air was warm, it was cooler than outside. The reception desk, made of weathered wood planks, sat to the left of a wide, sweeping staircase reminiscent of Gone with the Wind which rose from the flowered, carpeted lobby to disappear to the floors above.

A woman behind the desk cast her dispassionate gaze over them. The collar of her old-fashioned long-sleeved dress covered her long, narrow neck to just under her angular chin. Her hollow, sunken eyes were the color of obsidian and her complexion reminded Amanda of white glue. Maybe she's ill ....

"Hello," she said in a rasping voice. "May I help you?"

"Yes, ma'am," said Phillip, his tone musical and friendly—overly friendly; it sounded false to Amanda, and probably everyone else. She cringed inside. Regardless, he continued. "We need two rooms, please."

The old woman smirked, then flopped open a register, sending a puff of dust into air.

Amanda waved away the dust, blinking her eyes to clear them. "Two rooms?" she whispered to Phillip. "Why don't we share one? It'd be cheaper."

He turned his head slightly to look at her. "Best to have separate rooms." He grinned. "I might not be able to control myself."

Amanda offered a weak grin. I only wish. She immediately scolded herself. I'm acting like a lovesick schoolgirl; I'm a grown woman!

"How long have you been here?" Amanda asked the woman.

"All my life, Miss."

"Sorry, I meant, how long has the hotel been here?"

"Longer than I have."

Amanda studied the woman looking for signs she was joking, but she appeared to be serious, so Amanda shifted her gaze to look at Phillip. He offered her a humorless smile but didn't say anything.

After Phillip had signed the register for them both. After he'd signed them in the old woman placed two old-fashioned brass keys with yellowing paper tags attached to the ends on the desk. Her eyes dropped to peer at the two names Phillip had recorded in the ledger.

"Mr. Swann, I gave you room 212," she said. Her eyes shifted to

Amanda. "Room 312 for you, Miss Dark." The woman's tone was clipped and registered her disapproval of Amanda.

I guess she doesn't like questions.

"I'll carry your bag to your room," offered Phillip.

"No, thank you, Mr. Swann, I carry my own weight." Amanda snatched her room key off the desk; then, after grabbing her bag by the handle, hurried up the curved carpeted staircase to the guest rooms on the upper floors.

"I'll meet you here in the lobby in half an hour," Phillip called after her.

"OK." Without looking back, she hurried up the creaking stairs. She hoped they had Wi-Fi. The man and woman running the hotel seemed strangely out of place, though they claimed to have been living in Moonrise all their lives. She needed to conduct some research about the town and its remaining inhabitants.

THE FIRST THING she noticed upon entering the room was the smell. It reeked of mothballs and cigarette smoke. There was an old-fashioned gas lamp on an end table next to an antique burnished brass bed frame containing a too-soft mattress that sagged badly under the weight of her suitcase, which wasn't much since she'd packed light.

After tossing her suitcase on the bed, she set up her laptop on the cheap pine table set under the window overlooking the street in front of the hotel.

Moving the matching chair away from the desk, she sat down and flipped the laptop open. After booting it up she saw there was no Wi-Fi connection.

Disappointed, she next opened the folder with the pictures she'd downloaded of her uncle's diner from the family electronic archive her sister had set up years before, then clicked through them one by one. As she studied the photos, her mouth became dry and a lump of emotion grew in her throat as memories, both good and bad, washed over her.

She stopped clicking, the cursor now hovering over an image of Uncle Gib's diner back in the days he and Lucy had owned it, wondering if she'd overcome her fears and dread and be able to go inside. But she knew she had to; it was the only way she'd discover the truth.

Swiping the screen with her finger, the image of the pristine diner was replaced by a picture of the diner that had become severely dilapidated in the intervening decades, since it had been abandoned after her uncle's death.

Somehow, Amanda knew they'd discover the ghost of Lucy Dark haunting the old diner. When Lucy had died, her killer had never been brought to justice for her murder.

In Amanda's experience, this created the perfect paranormal recipe for spirits of the dead to be unable to cross over. Searching out Lucy's ghost seemed the only way to gain the information she and Phillip would need and perhaps to bring a killer to justice, putting an end to Lucy's wanderings.

The diner was now a severely neglected building, the wind and blowing sand having peeled most of the paint off the sign and the gray, weathered wood siding. There was a rusting 1940s pickup truck, the tires missing, sitting on blocks under all four wheels, beside the crumbling restaurant.

She traced the image of the diner on the screen with her index finger and sighed. At times like this, she wished the man who had once been her favorite uncle—something that until this moment she had forced herself to forget, had stayed as she remembered him ... before .... A sob escaped her lips; then she began to weep uncontrollably.

PHILLIP STOOD in the lobby facing the street, watching two tumble-weeds being pushed along by the constant desert wind. There were no signs of the old man or woman; he was alone. Dressed in tanned walking shorts, a navy blue golf shirt, and white Nikes, he had a pair of sunglasses raised high on his forehead.

"Hey, Amanda; ready to go?"

"Hi, Phillip," Amanda said, stepping off the last step of the staircase onto the worn oriental carpet.

Having changed into her exploration garb, she spun around, showing off her white walking shorts, mustard yellow blouse, and white open-toed sandals. "What do you think?"

Her unpleasant mood from when she'd last seen Phillip had disappeared. A good cry so often cleared out the cobwebs in her head. She hated being used; it ruined her day. It wasn't Phillip's fault her uncle had molested her; Phillip had treated her like a princess—he deserved better treatment.

Phillip turned toward her, smiling like the Cheshire cat. What was he up to now?

"You look good enough to take out on the town." He cocked one eyebrow. "Especially in this town."

He was joking of course, but she didn't really care where they went, provided they did it together. "Oh, Mr. Swann, you say the naughtiest things!"

He chuckled. "OK, Ms. Dark; let's go to the old diner and look for some clues. What do you say?"

She swallowed a sudden lump of fear in the back of her throat. "Sounds like a plan." She walked to stand beside him as he offered the crook of his arm. Grinning at him, she ran one hand around his offered arm.

~

AMANDA PLAYED the stream of white light emitted by the heavy-duty flashlight gripped in her sweaty, pale hand over the inky dark interior of the deserted roadside diner. Her heart beat hard in her chest; her dry mouth had a slightly metallic taste. Her tongue flicked over her lips.

She wondered where the ghost was hiding. It could be anywhere; in the walls, in the floor, in the kitchen cooking eggs …. She swallowed a chuckle. This was of course impossible. The power and water had been shut off after her uncle had died.

It had taken an hour to walk to the diner at the edge of town near the highway. Her feet hurt, and she was thirstier than she had ever been in her life; but Phillip seemed as fresh as when they'd set off. He wanted to continue, so she reluctantly agreed. Why couldn't they have brought the car?

When they'd arrived outside the diner, the sun had dropped to near the horizon. It would be dark in an hour. The doors and windows of the diner were boarded up, but together they managed to pry the ones off the front door to get inside; not that it was all that difficult, since the wooden boards and the wood door were dry and badly rotted by the desert conditions over the past two decades of neglect. Once inside, they'd had to use flashlights in order to see.

"We don't get a lot of customers these days," said a woman's voice coming from their right.

A six-foot section of counter—a section of which appeared to be have crumbled away due to rot—and six rusted, round steel stools in front were all that remained of the original lunch counter. The fabric of the booths' seats beside the boarded-up windows across was dusty and ripped, the stuffing hanging out in great clumps, as if torn apart by wild animals.

The voice continued, "Not since they built the bypass."

"The bypass was built in 1962," whispered Phillip in Amanda's ear.

Amanda realized that the voice must belong to Gib's first wife.

"Uhhh, Lucy? Is that you?" Swinging her flashlight beam she discovered a woman standing behind the counter, a waitress dressed in a pink uniform skirt and matching blouse. Her fiery red curls were partially covered by a little white-trimmed pink hat; in one hand, she held a green and white order pad, in the other, a glass carafe filled with black coffee. Steam actually rose from inside the carafe.

The waitress — obviously a ghost, as evidenced by her pale ivory complexion and unblinking stare—wore a sardonic smile on her bloodless lips, her pale green eyes reflecting curiosity.

"Yes; are you two cops or sumthin'?" Lucy's ghost didn't wait for a response; instead, she grunted, then took a step farther down the dusty counter away from them. She poured a measure of coffee into a dusty white china mug on the counter.

Amanda assumed Lucy could see whoever was seated at the counter, but that she herself couldn't. It was an odd restriction of her gift, something she had experienced a few times before; certain ghosts left behind echoes of the host after the spirit itself had crossed over. It happened maybe one in twenty-six times, so while it wasn't that common, she had seen it before.

Lucy's ghost recognized these echoes and thought they were as 'real' as herself; ghosts were unable to discern echoes from other ghosts. This particular echo must have been a customer of the diner.

"Why don't you cops move along and stop bothering old Barney and me. "Ain't that right, Barney?" Lucy winked at the empty stool in front of the counter.

"Uhhh, Lucy—" began Amanda.

Lucy's ghost set the carafe on the counter and turned to silence Amanda with a glare, and Phillip; both had their flashlights trained on her. "Do I know you people?" Amanda shook her head. "Then how do you know my name?"

Amanda hesitated. It was a good question, and one that deserved a response. "Well, you see I'm Gib Dark's niece—"

Lucy's features were suddenly split by a wide grin and she rushed to stand in front of Amanda, the ghostly figure now sparkling under the light from the two flashlights.

"You're Mandy?" Lucy spoke excitedly. "Well, why didn't you say so when you came in?" Lucy turned to look at the pass bar beyond which was the kitchen. "Hey, Gib, Mandy's here!"

Amanda froze; her hands trembled, causing the flashlight beam to shake, and her heart beat rapidly in her chest. The swinging door separating the counter from the kitchen hung at an angle on one hinge. He'd have to pass through the wall ....

A sudden wave of dizziness gripped her. Reaching out to grip the edge of the counter in order to steady herself made the beam of light to wave about wildly. Phillip's flashlight also swung about crazily, so she knew he was experiencing the same thing as her.

The feeling quickly passed, but from the corner of one eye Amanda saw the diner had started to change physically. Amanda's heart skipped a beat. The diner was transforming, somehow reverting to a past time when it had been new.

"Impossible," she whispered under her breath.

The weathered gray wall, the paint peeling from the crumbling plaster farthest away, straightened and became smooth, then changed from gray to a mint green. Next, the section of the counter that had been missing reappeared as if from nothing.

The white-gray speckled linoleum tiles on the floor looked freshly waxed. The light fixtures lining the ceiling changed from broken and rusted to gleaming stainless steel with glowing bulbs. The light fixtures, too, now looked to be newly installed.

As the wave touched the stools in front of the counter, they began to change from rusting relics to shiny new under the glow of the lights. Even the seat fabric of the booths against the windows and the stools, now a shiny aquamarine color, appeared to be brand new with not one tear or mark.

Like a fast moving tsunami, the changes spread across the diner, racing toward them unrelenting and undulating as if alive. As the wave of change was about to engulf them, Amanda closed her eyes and held her breath.

Nothing happened for several seconds, but she was too afraid to move.

"Hey, Mandy, what's wrong?" Uncle Gib?

The soft burr of an air conditioner motor sent a gentle breeze of cold air over her. When they'd first walked in, the musty collapsing diner had been too warm and too humid. After releasing the air from her lungs, she sucked in a breath of the cool air. It felt so good.

Opening one eye she saw a much younger version than she remembered of her Uncle Gib, coming toward her from the kitchen through the now brand new swinging door. With his square jaw and dark wavy hair, he looked as real and solid as if he were still alive. The man was grinning.

Sucking in another breath, she closed her eyes again as she struggled to steady her nerves. The transformation of an environment had never happened before during a paranormal investigation; it was too incredible, too unbelievable to be real, but it was real.

How is this possible?

She opened both eyes to find herself looking into the coal black pupils of the man who had molested her. This man was her Uncle Gib.

~

SEATED AT THE LUNCH COUNTER, her bottom resting on the soft cushion, Amanda sipped from the clean glass of water she held in her trembling fingers. Phillip sat on the stool beside her, sipping clear water from an identical glass. Her scream of shock still seemed to echo off the restaurant's walls.

Lucy and Gib stood leaning back against the waist-high fridges beneath the service counter built into the wall behind them. To their right, in the wall, was an opening with a stainless-steel pass bar where prepared food was placed to await pick-up by a waitress. Three heat lamps ran along the top edge of the opening, shining down on the pass bar to keep the orders warm until they were picked up.

As if Amanda's aunt and uncle weren't in the room, Phillip asked her to explain the transformation of the diner's interior, but she was unable to offer any explanation since she'd never seen this happen before. It surprised her that he was able to see it happen, too. This was way beyond her experience or expertise and, she was afraid to admit, it frightened her.

The diner now looked brand new, as if they were no longer in 2014, but had been transported back to 1957. Time travel was impossible, so she concluded this was some sort of paranormal event unlike anything she'd ever witnessed.

"Ummm," she began, her voice tentative, "Uncle Gib, did you build the diner?"

Uncle Gib focused his black eyes on her and nodded. "Yes, me and Lucy did all the work ourselves, with our own two hands." His eyes were humorless, and his tanned forehead was marred by a frown.

After the diner had regenerated—Amanda decided that the word 'regenerated' best described what they'd witnessed—Gib and Lucy became fully human again, though in their younger bodies. They looked as real and alive as Amanda and Phillip; even their cheeks were flushed, as if they had blood in their veins.

Amanda's well-tuned sense for all things paranormal told her that when they left the diner, it would revert to its former dilapidated condition. She wished she had an explanation for all this that made some sense.

My gift really messes with my head some days.

Fortunately, she'd seen enough weird things on this job that one more strange, unexpected happening eventually had come to seem actually normal on some level.

"I'm so sorry, Uncle Gibb," she said, finally able to look her uncle in the eyes.

Gib shrugged, but neither Lucy nor him looked unhappy. "You scared away all our customers," blurted Lucy. "We have bills to pay, ya know."

Gib shifted his gaze to his wife and placed one hand on her shoulder. "Take it easy, honey. Mandy's always been high strung."

As if struck by a bolt from a blue sky, an idea suddenly occurred to Amanda. "If this is the fifties, then I haven't been born yet. How would you know what I'm like?"

Gib winced. Grinning sheepishly, he said, "I don't know, Mandy. I have access to all of the memories from my corporeal existence. Even .... " His voice trailed off as his cheeks flushed crimson.

A familiar tingle of anger swelled in Amanda's belly, but she forced it down. Anger would only lead to more pain; now that she had him in front of her, she might finally get the answers she'd been seeking all her life. "Yes, of course .... I'm curious about your death and Lucy's—" She stopped, uncertain if she should break the news of Lucy's murder to the victim.

Lucy slammed a fist into Gib's shoulder, causing him to wince in pain. "How does she know about that?" Gibb shrugged.

I guess she knows already. "It's OK, Lucy," Amanda said, "After my father's death, I found an envelope in his files containing a letter Gib wrote." She eyed her uncle, who appeared very much alive. Death seemed a debatable concept right now, so she decided not to tell Lucy about Gib's suicide. She sensed that Lucy didn't know everything about her husband, which actually made sense since she'd died before Gib had crawled into a whiskey bottle, and before he'd molested Amanda.

"Anyway, regardless of our present circumstance, I know, Lucy, you were murdered, based on the contents of Uncle Gib's letter. He claims he was an undercover operative for the Arizona State Police and that someone was sending him a message by killing you."

Gib nodded, his head dropping to his chest. "She's right." His voice was barely audible.

Lucy's pale features twisted in anger as she raised her fist and hit him in the shoulder again, this time harder than before. "You son of a .... You used me ...! Milt killed me, didn't he?" Gib groaned and wrapped his injured arm with his left hand. "Didn't he!" Lucy arms were at her sides with her hands curled into fists.

Gib nodded but remained silent.

"Uhhh, who's, Milt?' asked Amanda. She thought about asking about the gangsters mentioned in the trial transcript, but she wanted to hear this first.

Lucy looked at her. "Milt was his partner on the police force. I've never met anyone so jealous as that pig." She shuddered. "An awful man, crude, drank too much .... He craved violence, ya know?"

"Was this before or after you started the diner?' asked Phillip.

Lucy stepped away from her cowed husband, crossing her arms over her chest. "Not that it matters now, but Gib started this diner to escape his old job as a cop." She shifted her eyes to glare at Gib, who avoided her. "We were tired of the danger, the late nights, no days off, his crazy partner, ... all of it. Frankly, if Gib didn't leave the state police we were through."

"Where can we find this Milt?" asked Phillip.

Gib looked at Amanda through bloodshot eyes. "Milton Spender lives in a nursing home in Phoenix." Her uncle looked so sad she couldn't help but feel sorry for him. But, before dealing with the problem with Lucy, she needed to air some family laundry.

"Uncle Gib ...," she began; the old dark fear rising from within her closed her throat. Pushing it aside, she continued. "Uncle Gib, why did you molest me?"

He stuffed his hands in the pockets of his white cook pants while avoiding her eyes. "I'm so sorry, Mandy. I was drunk. I had a problem." He hesitated. "I told your father what happened, promising never to return to Boston." He locked eyes with her, his filled with tears. "I know it's not an acceptable excuse, but please, please forgive me. I've loved you like the daughter I never had since I first saw you at the hospital when you were born."

His eyes pleaded with her for forgiveness. Slowly the fear that had consumed her life, the shame that had permeated her soul since she was twelve years old began to recede. After more than two decades, a terrible burden lifted from her shoulders.

She looked at Phillip, hoping that he might help her to decide, but since he hadn't known how badly her uncle had hurt her until this moment, he couldn't really help; he hadn't lived with this terrible secret. He gazed at her with sad eyes, a weak smile on his lips. While she sensed Phillip's sympathy, only she could decide.

"Alright, Uncle Gib ...." Her words caught in her throat, and a shiver ran down her spine, but she pushed herself through the fear. "I'll ... forgive you ...."

A sudden feeling of pure joy shot from her toes to her head; her words had set her free from the past. Her paranormal senses tingled, signaling she had done the correct thing by forgiving someone who had so impacted her life.

Gib buried his head in his hands and began to sob while Lucy stroked his back. She looked at Amanda. "Thank you," she said softly.

Turning away, Phillip wrapped Amanda in his arms, pulled her to him, and stroked her shoulder. She rested her head against his chest feeling the steady beating of his heart against her.

"We have to visit this Milton Spender," she said. "Lucy needs our help."

Phillip chuckled lightly. "That's my girl, always thinking of others." He released her and grasped her shoulders with both hands gazing into her eyes. "How're you doing?"

"I've never felt better in my life," she said, and meant it.

UPON DRIVING through the iron gates of the retirement community where Milton Spender lived, Amanda saw nothing like the retirement homes she'd seen before, or even imagined a retirement community could be. The sprawling, perfectly manicured facilities had to be exclusive to the very, very rich. No one of middle class means could afford such a place, so how a retired cop would be living in such a community ...?

Designed around a massive park with sprawling flower beds of roses, gardenias, and mature rhododendrons covered with red, white and yellow flowers, bordered tennis courts, an Olympic-sized pool, and even a full eighteen hole golf course. The magnificent grounds reminded Amanda more of a five-star resort than a place where old folks went to die.

Amanda had forgotten to ask Uncle Gib about the gangsters, but decided it was too thin a line to follow since Lucy and Gib seemed adamant that Milt Spender was the killer. Still, something niggled at the back of her mind, telling her something wasn't right, but she couldn't put a finger on what was bothering her.

After parking under the breezeway covering the entrance, Amanda, with Phillip by her side, entered the lobby through the twin glass doors after a female valet took the keys for their rental car, saying she would park it for them.

The lobby smelled of lemon floor polish, gleaming marble tiles covering the floor, finally ending at the massive reception desk. Behind the desk sat a man with slicked-back black hair cut close to his large head, wearing a white nurse's uniform. As they approached the desk, Amanda spotted a name tag over his left breast pocket that read 'C. Reddick'.

Forcing her best glad-to-meet-you smile on her lips as they arrived at the desk, she said, "Hello. We're looking for Milton Spender."

Reddick, whose black eyes had been focused on a document on the desk, looked up at them. "Milt? Why would you want ta see that old son of a bitch?"

Startled for a few seconds that Reddick would speak of a resident this way, Amanda waited several seconds before speaking. "Uhhh, well, we have an old friend who knows Milt and wants us to check in on him." Her mouth formed a weak smile. "To see if he's okay."

Reddick snorted derisively and rose from the chair he'd been sitting in. "It's your funeral, lady." He walked to stand in front of a bulletin board affixed to the wall behind him. After scanning a document pegged to the board, he said, "Milt should be in the music appreciation class. That is, if he felt like it today." He grunted. "Every day's an adventure, with Milt."

Shaking his head, he walked back to sit in the chair. "Got ID?"

Phillip pulled out his wallet while Amanda opened her purse and extracted her driver's license from a pocket inside. After Reddick had looked over their identification, he asked them to sign their names in a visitor's register.

"Folks from Boston come all the way to Phoenix to see a bastard like Milt Spender ...." He snorted again. "Makes no difference to me, but you've come a long way for nuthin'." He handed them each a fire-engine red plasticized visitor's pass with a clip-to for them to attach it to their breast pockets, instructing them to display them at all times while on the premises.

"Thank you, Mr. Reddick. Which way to the class?"

Reddick pointed to the wide hallway left of the desk filled with older men and women shuffling along aided by walkers, some in wheel chairs, others in track suits walking briskly along, their sport shoes squeaking on the tiled floor. To a person, they all appeared happy and content. "Follow the yellow line on the wall to G Wing, Room 128A."

Amanda turned to face Phillip. Lowering her voice so Reddick couldn't hear them, she said, "Why don't you find a place for a coffee? I want to speak with Mr. Spender by myself." Phillip opened his mouth to speak until she placed one finger over his lips. "No questions, please. I need to do this alone."

Phillip nodded, but his eyes told her he wasn't happy about her decision. Nevertheless, he disappeared in the opposite direction after asking a passing nurse directions to the cafeteria.

Amanda watched him go, her stomach jumping to its own beat since her nerves were on edge. This case had given her a nervous stomach. She hadn't been sleeping well since starting the trek to Arizona and meeting her uncle and aunt's younger ghosts hadn't helped her condition. True, a major emotional weight had been lifted from her after she'd forgiven Gib, but she had the sinking feeling that this visit to Milt wasn't going to end well.

She made her way along the maze of hallways, following the yellow line painted on wall until she found G Wing. A sign with arrows under the big letter G showed that room 128A was to the left.

Taking in a deep breath, she headed down the hallway, letting the air escape her lungs and taking another deep breath as she walked. She passed a number of the white-haired residents, all of whom nodded as they offered her close-mouthed smiles. With all the smiling, Amanda began to wonder if this was the Stepford senior's home and all these people were duplicates created by computers and microchips.

The nurses she passed, on the other hand, didn't even look in her direction, causing her to wonder about the effectiveness of the security system. In Amanda's line of work, you tended to look at the details of a place when entering unknown territory. Often, the minutiae of a place told you more than the people or the larger, more elaborate details.

Staff who ignored the most basic security protocols showed they couldn't care less about the place where they worked or its residents, or the security personnel were incompetent, lazy, or both.

Sure enough, a portly man appeared from around a corner, coming in her direction wearing a white shirt with shoulder patches reading 'Security' and black slacks. His blond hair was cut to half an inch from his round head. He rode a Segway. Dark sunglasses hid his eyes and the belt around his waist was heavy with all sorts of rattling tools in numerous leather pouches.

As he rolled to a stop beside her, he gazed at her. The portable radio on his belt was on a low volume, but she could still hear snatches of conversations; something about a big game of some kind, and someone else talking about what they were making for dinner that night.

"Hey, there, Miss; you got a visitor pass?"

Amanda showed him the visitor badge clipped to the hem of her shirt.

"OK, thank you, Miss." He nodded, then headed away, soon disappearing in an adjacent hallway.

Watching the security guard until he disappeared, she finally shook head. "Yup, that's a poor excuse for security. You called it, girl," she murmured.

Finally, she found room 128A and, after opening the door, stuck her head inside. The room was large; no doubt it could seat at least fifty people at tables and chairs comfortably. There were no windows, and the walls were lined with billboards from famous Broadway shows.

At the front of the room was a row of five occupied wheelchairs in front of which was a raised platform, upon which a rail-thin brown-haired man stood beside a small table where a mini-stereo blared music. Amanda recognized the tune being played.

It was a song from the Broadway musical Oklahoma, the one about the fringe on top, or something like that. Her dad had loved those musicals and played the cast albums all the time when she was a young girl. But, right now, she had more important things to take care of, like catching a murderer and helping two ghosts pass over.

One of the occupants of the wheelchairs had to be Milt Spender.

Stepping inside, she closed the door as softly as possible so as not to disturb the audience's enjoyment of the show tunes echoing off the walls. She walked as softly as possible toward the platform until she stood behind the wheelchairs, the occupants of which were exclusively male.

How am I going to nail down which one is Spender without interrupting the class?

It was then that she noticed that the man on the platform was glaring at her, his brow marred by deep creases. He was trying to get her attention by mouthing something she didn't understand. She raised her hands in mock surrender and shrugged.

Walking around to stand in front of the wheelchairs she studied each grizzled man. Two were thin, two were heavy, and one was medium. The three bears of the seniors set.

One had a scar on his left cheek, one had wispy gray hair that touched his shoulders, and one was bald as a cue ball. Her nose wrinkled at the overpowering odor of garlic emanating from the 'cue ball'.

The man at the end of the row glared at her with red-rimmed azure eyes. Unshaven, wearing a dirty, red and brown plaid night gown over sky blue pajamas, his bare feet resting on the foot rests of the wheelchair, he seemed the most likely candidate to be a retired cop. His eyes followed her as she walked toward him. Yup, cop.

"Milt?" she whispered after stepping up to stand over him.

He grimaced. "What the fuck do you want?"

His tone suggested aggression, but his hands, buried in his lap, were trembling. And his head wobbled like a bobble head. Minutiae reveals truth.

"Let's you and I get out of here, Milt. We need to talk." She sensed that all she needed to do was push him a little harder and he'd be putty in her hands.

Milt avoided her steady gaze. "I'm not going anywhere with you, bitch." He spat the words from between his cracked, dry lips, but his words lacked forcefulness.

She moved so she stood in front of him again, but he snapped his head in the other direction as if trying to escape. "Really?" she said. "Would you prefer we conducted our business in here?"

Milt's eyes shifted to lock with hers; there was fear behind them. "No ..., I mean ..., not really ...." He reached down to unlock the brake on his chair then began to wheel away, using his hands to push the tires forward.

She glanced at the man on the platform and nodded. He raised the middle finger of his left hand to flash her what her father used to call flipping-the-bird, a universal insult. What a nice guy.

Amanda followed Milt out the door to the corridor, then down the hall until they arrived at a door with a picture of him, his name written underneath in block letters. The picture of him looked pretty much identical to the man seated in the wheelchair.

Milt slapped a stainless-steel plate on the wall next to the door and it began to open slowly into the room. As the gap became wider, the fluorescent lights in the ceiling inside flickered to life.

When the door had opened sufficiently, Milt turned his head slightly to catch her eye, grunted, then turned to face forward and rolled himself inside. Amanda followed him in, watching him until he stopped at the window overlooking the golf course where, in the distance, one gray-haired man was striking his golf ball while another man of a similar vintage watched from a powered cart.

It was sunny outside, but Milt's room was located under an overhang, so very little sunlight came through the window.

Milt's elbows rested on the wheelchair's armrests, his hands in front of him, clasping, unclasping, worrying themselves with nervous energy. He peered at the golfers, his body trembling uncontrollably. "I always knew this day would come," he said, his voice soft as sun-warmed butter. "Are you going to kill me now?"

Amanda snorted, causing him to look at her, surprise registering on his gaunt, unshaven features. "Milt, I'm not here to kill you. I'm here to help Lucy and Gib Dark."

Milt shifted his bottom in his wheelchair. "Gib? Lucy? They're—"

"Dead," she finished for him. "Yes, they are; but their ghosts are very much still around, and they don't want to be around, for lack of a term that would make some sense to a lay person such as yourself."

Milt had stopped shaking, the fear beginning to dissipate. "Sorry, I don't follow ...."

She nodded and moved to sit on the single bed facing him. "Gib claims you killed his wife, Lucy. I need to know if you did." She leaned toward him, her eyes on his. "It's just that easy." Now that she was closer, she detected the sour smell of sweat coming from Milt. She wondered when was the last time he'd bathed.

Gib was gaining confidence now, his arrogance returning. "I used to be a cop, ya know."

She smirked. "Yes, I know. You were Gib's partner." She looked out the window. "From the look of this place, I'd say you were a corrupt cop."

Milt's eyes narrowed. "How would you know?"

Amanda chuckled. "Let's stop playing games, Milty; just answer my question. Did you murder Lucy Dark?"

"Lady, I have no idea who the fuck you are, so I'm not gonna tell you shit."

"From what I see, Milt, my boy, you may need my services sooner than later."

"Oh, yeah, really? So, who and what are you, that a useless old man like me would require your services?"

Amanda grinned. "I'm Amanda Dark, I'm Gib's niece and I'm a paranormal investigator. I also have a special talent helping spirits of the dead unable to cross over after their death due to unresolved issues while they were alive." The grin faded from her lips and she turned her attention to Milt. "You're dying. From your appearance, I'd say most likely cancer."

Milt's eyes went wide and watery. "How did you know?"

"I know all, I see all, sorta like a modern-day Wizard of Oz, only I don't hide behind a curtain." She paused to consider her next words; then, she had an idea.

"Listen, Milt, I'll make you a deal. If you tell me who killed Lucy, I'll help you cross over when the time comes."

One corner of Milt's mouth curled slightly. "Who said I'd have any problem crossing over?"

"Trust me, Milt, I'm a professional. I always know." Amanda paused to wait for Milt to mull over her offer. Truth was she had no idea if he'd have problems; she didn't know enough about him. She'd made her offer on the scant bits of details she'd gleaned after meeting him, her special intuition, and what Gib and Lucy had said about him.

It wasn't much to go on, but she was betting that even if she missed the mark, she'd at least have nicked a corner of truth.

Milt might not actually want to go wherever it was he was headed after death if he was a crooked cop and a murderer. In her experience, the afterlife was never what people expected, or so her spirit contacts had told her.

Milt moved his wheelchair slightly back from the window, the tires making a soft burr sound on the tiles. His head hung down to his chest. "OK, but please help me. I've done some stuff I'm not proud of ...." His voice dropped off and a gasp escaped his lips. He looked up into her eyes as trails made by tears ran down his sunken cheeks.

Her heart ached for him. This man suffered from terrible, soul-crushing pain. She resolved to help him, no matter what it took.

"Why don't you tell me everything," she said softly.

In a halting voice, Milt began his story.

Amanda listened, intent on his words filled with raw emotion concerning things he obviously hadn't talked about in a very long time.

She was right about his terminal cancer. Since Milt was nearing his eighty-ninth birthday, he'd already accepted the inevitable end.

He assured Amanda that he hadn't killed Lucy. Though he was jealous of Gib and thought Lucy was too good for his partner, he couldn't hurt either of them. Years after Gib had left the police force, Milt and his new partner had been offered substantial bribes from drug dealers to look the other way.

Since his finances had been wiped out in a real estate scam and his wife had left him, he'd decided that he deserved to retire in style, so he'd accepted the offers and had managed to accrue a significant amount of money. "I was wrong. Money isn't what's important in life," he said.

He then explained that while he hadn't killed Lucy, he knew who did, but had been threatened with exposure of his corruption if he ever revealed the truth. He'd remained silent since that time.

Amanda's heart rate increased. Now she was getting somewhere. "Who wanted to send Gib a message by murdering his wife?"

Milt looked down at the floor. "That's what he always believed, but it wasn't true. The killer wasn't sending him any message ...." His voice caught.

"OK, so if that wasn't the motive, then why?"

Milt sighed, his breath shaky. "Someone wanted Lucy for themselves ..., someone powerful ..., dangerous. When Gib and Lucy said no, he threatened to kill her."

"Who?"

He looked up at her through bloodshot eyes. He opened his mouth to speak, but the intercom speaker in the ceiling cut him off. The announcer's voice was feminine, nasal, and slightly annoying. "Residents, there are now lemon cookies and green tea available in the cafeteria, where we will be starting the bingo game shortly. So join your fellow residents for a fun-filled afternoon."

As the announcer spoke, Amanda stood and walked to the window overlooking the golf course, her shoes scuffing over the tile. Watching two new golfers swinging at their balls reminded her what a silly game golf really was.

When announcer had finished, she shifted her eyes to look at Milt and froze. His face was the color of a concord grape; he was gasping for breath, his gnarled hands clasping at his throat.

Her heart beating rapidly, Amanda searched frantically for the call button to summon assistance. Finally, her eyes landed on a panel on the wall with three colored buttons over the single bed crammed into an alcove. She hurried to the panel and pressed the black button marked NURSES STATION. Nothing happened.

There was a speaker on the panel under the buttons. The label under the blue button to the left of the black button said it was for the intercom. Pressing the button and holding it in, Amanda shouted into the speaker. "Help! I need help!"

After she released the button, a man's sluggish voice replied. "Alright, lady, take it easy."

"No, you don't understand ...." Milt had begun to make choking noises, and he shuddered as air rushed from his lungs, then his eyes rolled back in his head.

Amanda froze, her eyes wide with horror as Milt's gnarled hands frantically undid the seat belt holding him in the chair. He tried to stand, but instead he slumped forward until he finally collapsed to the floor, first onto his knees, until he dropped on his belly, his face bouncing off the tiles with his arms and legs sprawled out from his torso, bent at unnatural angles.

Milton Spender was dead.

AMANDA JOINED Phillip in the cafeteria where he sat alone at one end of a table large enough for ten people, a cinnamon bun and a white ceramic mug in front of him. Amanda was relieved that there were very few people in the cafeteria at this time of day since it was just after two o'clock in the afternoon. The last thing she needed was for anyone to overhear their conversation and then have to explain it. Most people did not understand or appreciate her work.

She could see that a few bites were missing from the cinnamon bun but that the remainder remained untouched. The mug, which she saw contained black coffee, was half empty; or was it half full?

"No good?" she asked, nodding at the bun after sitting in an empty chair across from Phillip.

"Terrible," he said. "Dry as the dust in a vacuum cleaner bag, and the icing is so sweet it hurts your teeth." He shrugged and raised the mug to his lips to take a sip. "Coffee's okay, though."

"Milt's dead."

Phillip had raised his mug again, intending to take another drink of coffee, but he stopped a few inches from his mouth, the mug floating. "What? How?"

"He was terminal." She shrugged. "It was just a matter of time."

Looking away so he couldn't see the sadness in her eyes, she cleared her throat. The truth was she'd never gotten used to death, no matter how much she experienced in her job. And Milt's end had been truly terrible.

She secretly hoped she never would, since helping the dead had been her motivation to become a paranormal investigator in the first place.

"Wow," said Phillip, before he took a generous drink of coffee and then set the mug on the table. "Did he say anything important before he died?"

She nodded, still avoiding him. "He said someone else wanted Lucy for themselves, and when she wouldn't agree, he threatened to kill her."

"So, who was this person?"

Amanda turned to face him and sighed. "He was about to tell me when ...."

Phillip snorted, and his mouth formed a crooked smile. "Yeah, he was cut off just like in the movies. I'm surprised there wasn't a knife sticking from his back."

"A man is dead, Phillip; this is no time for jokes."

Phillip winced. "Yeah, I'm sorry, Amanda, but death makes me a little goofy. I'll stop. But really, any idea who he might have been talking about?"

She nodded, her eyes drifting to the vacant chair next to him, then moving back to him. "Actually, there were several gangsters mentioned in the trial transcript Gib they said may have been the murderer."

Phillip arched a single eyebrow. "Really? Any idea which one Milt might have known?"

"Oh, I expect he knew them all, but his ghost told me the name of one who was jealous of Gib and who'd threatened Lucy."

"Well, why didn't you say so before?"

"Because, my dear Phillip, Milt's ghost just sat down beside you and shared the name with me."

Phillip chuckled. Since partnering with Amanda on several cases, nothing shocked him anymore and he fully accepted that her talents were very real. "I love it when you use your gift. It really is so cool."

Amanda grinned. "Thanks, partner. We're going to find Al 'Stinky' Garbone, the man who allegedly murdered Lucy Dark."

She knew then she wouldn't need to find Stinky Al, because the murder of Lucy had been pure cause and effect. Amanda's paranormal senses told her that something was rotten in Arizona. Neither Milt nor this faceless small-time wise guy, Stinky Al, had killed Lucy. She knew now who'd committed the murder and who should pay the price.

Amanda entered the Moonrise Diner with Phillip one step behind her. Upon seeing the diner's interior, she pulled up short, and he ran into her from behind, nearly causing her to stumble and fall. "Hey! Watch it."

"Sorry," Phillip said, after stepping away from her. "What's up?"

"Look at this place," Amanda said waving her arms at the pile of wood wreckage around them. It actually seemed worse than before.

Phillip scanned the restaurant. "Yeah, it looks like an old, dumpy, broken-down diner."

Amanda had never expected to find the diner shiny and new like when they'd left it last time, but the dilapidated condition of the long-abandoned building caught her off guard. Dust and mold covered every shattered booth and the rotting counters were weathered, and sand had blown in through the gaping holes in the walls.

She hadn't realized how bad it was inside before, since it had been dark the last time they'd been there. In the daytime, she worried that the ceiling would fall on them any second. This wasn't so much a haunted diner as a 'had-it' diner.

"Uhhh, Uncle Gib? Aunt Lucy?" Amanda stepped forward tentatively, unsure if the floor might collapse beneath her at any second. She froze when the floorboard under her creaked, followed by a loud snapping sound.

Suddenly, the broken-down restaurant began to transform once again, beginning at the far wall.

Amanda closed her eyes as the wave of change came rushing toward her. Her heart pounded hard in her chest. Within seconds, there was a soft whirr, then a cool breeze washed over her. Opening one eye, she saw a smiling Gib standing behind the transformed lunch counter beside Lucy, who also grinned at her.

"Whew," she said, "I'm so glad to see you two." Amanda collapsed with relief on an empty stool while Phillip sat on the one next to her. She shot him a glance and saw that his eyes looked as relieved as she felt. The diner had been regenerated before it fell on them.

"Do you have good news?" asked Gib, his handsome face eager as a child on his birthday.

"Sort of," began Amanda, uncertain how Gib and Lucy would

accept the death of Gib's old partner. Much like taking off a Band-Aid, it was best to do it in one go. "Milt's dead."

Gib's face sagged. "Really?"

Amanda nodded. "But I did manage to speak to him while he was still alive."

"So, you killed him?" said Lucy, as she wiped the counter with a white cloth.

"No, of course not, I don't kill people. I just talk to dead people." She hesitated, realizing how ridiculous this sounded. But then, Gib and Lucy were ghosts, and she was talking to them ....

Gib glanced at Lucy. "Why don't you get them some coffee?" Lucy nodded and walked to the stainless-steel coffee-brewer station standing on the service counter in front of the wall separating the kitchen from the counter area. The brewer had three warmers, each with a glass carafe containing black coffee. The two on the side warmers were half full; the one under the dispensing spout was three quarters full.

Ghosts must drink a lot of coffee.

Lucy filled two white ceramic mugs, then came back to set them on the lunch counter in front of them. "I'll get the creamer and the sugar," she said. She quickly returned with a stainless-steel creamer with a hinged lid, a mint-green ceramic bowl filled with white sugar, and two spoons.

Phillip looked at Amanda, his eyes curious. She shrugged, then reached to grasp the mug and realized it was warm. Raising the mug, she sipped the coffee, and it tasted slightly nutty and rich. How was this possible?

Lucy looked anxious. "Is it OK?"

Amanda nodded. "Yeah, it's good." Phillip raised his mug and took a small sip. His eyes went wide.

Amanda grinned and set the mug back on the counter. "As I was saying, I spoke to Milt, and he told me who really murdered Lucy." Seeing the fear in Gib's ghostly eyes, she paused. It seemed that every case brought new experiences. A ghost, afraid? Who knew?

She cleared her throat, then continued. "Anyway, Milt said some guy named Stinky Al murdered Lucy—"

"I knew it!" Gib cut her off and turned to face his wife. "You and Al? Really?"

Lucy took two steps back from Gib, her body trembling, fear in her eyes. "Gib, it wasn't like that ...."

Gib walked up to her and pressed an index finger into her chest. "Really? You and Al were cheating on me behind my back, weren't you? You lousy whore! Slut!" It was then that Amanda realized that Gib had a chef's knife gripped in his right hand. He stepped up and slashed the blade across Lucy's throat.

Since she was a ghost, her head separated from her body, floating in mid-air, but no blood came from the wound. "Gib!" Lucy's disembodied head screamed at her husband. "You bastard! You killed me again!"

Amanda leaned closer to Phillip in order not to be heard. "I think it's time we exited stage left."

Phillip raised one eyebrow. "Huh?"

"Let's go and leave these two lovebirds alone."

They rose simultaneously from the stools and hurried to the door just as the diner began to revert to its former state of about-to-collapse.

Once outside, they watched as the diner's four walls collapsed inward with a loud crash. Then the roof fell onto the pile of broken, weather-grayed wood, enveloping them in a cloud of dust and sand. The diner was now a pile of kindling.

"What just happened?" asked Phillip, coughing as the dust cloud settled over them. Trying in vain to brush off his tan shorts and cactus green shirt, he turned to face Amanda, who shook her head to shake some of the dust out of her hair.

She snorted to clear her nostrils and spat sand from her

mouth. "The end of the Moonrise Diner, obviously, but also the truth."

"What truth?"

"Gib killed Lucy and got away with it, blaming Milt, then Stinky Al. They were decoys, or maybe an excuse to fool himself or to bury his guilt, or who knows why. Whatever the reasons, my Uncle Gib is exactly who he appeared to be."

"What now?"

Amanda smirked. "Well, I expect with the destruction of the diner they've both crossed over." She scanned the wreckage. "Somehow I don't think Gib is much liking where he ended up."

Phillip stepped up and wrapped his arms around her. She hugged him back, feeling his heart beating against her chest. "What about you?" he said softly.

"I'm better. Much better."

Whoever said The truth will set you free. knew exactly what they were talking about, because Amanda Dark had never felt as free as she did right now.

# A FATHER'S DAUGHTER

*An Amanda Dark story time told from the point of view of her spectral client. A tale where personal stakes take a horrifying twist.*

Saffron shifted her bottom on the hard pine chair, where she sat studying the unadorned steel-gray walls and floor of her ten-by-ten-foot surroundings the burnished steel desk in the center of the otherwise bare room. Looking down at herself, she discovered that she was dressed in black slacks, flats, and a white cotton long-sleeved shirt. The clothes reminded her of the K-Mart housewives she silently mocked when she made trips to the mall to visit the high-end shops for new shoes and the latest fashions. She had closets reserved just for her shoes. She had never worn such frumpy clothes in her life.

Seated across from her in a brown, well-worn leather chair was a pale-faced, severe-looking woman with mint-green eyes, her angular features focused on the pages of a large clothbound book open on the desk in front of her.

Saffron had no sense of how long, or even how, she'd been

here or. But she did have a vague sense of unease, deep in her belly, that had formed a knot reminiscent of hunger.

Yet, she wasn't hungry—at least not exactly as she thought of hunger. In the recesses of her mind, memories of the taste of champagne and cherries and coffee bubbled, but she felt no compulsion or need for them. Something had changed. But what?

Saffron's auburn eyes finally landed on the woman across from her, who smelled of peppermints and chamomile tea, like her grandmother who had died when she and her twin sister, Sadie, had been fifteen years old. Their father had taken them with him to retrieve her grandmother's clothes for the funeral. She recalled seeing the hairbrush lying face up on her grandmother's antique mirrored dresser, the battleship-gray wisps of hair still clinging to the stiff, black horsehair bristles as if trapped for eternity as the only remaining evidence of the woman who had given her chocolate candies at Christmas and sent crisp new dollar bills for her and her sister in a birthday card each year.

A twinge of regret for her unkindness toward her elderly grandmother invaded her thoughts briefly, then retreated immediately. As far back as she could recall, her grandmother had been trapped in a frail body twisted by painful arthritis. Saffron had been young and stupid then, a horribly self-absorbed teenager who had failed to appreciate her elders.

But her deepest regret was reserved for her father, whose angry eyes had bored into her when, at her grandmother's funeral, she and her sister had giggled at some inane private joke between them.

Mercifully, he'd never spoken to her about the incident, but she knew they had disappointed him. Her beloved father was the only man she had ever looked to for wisdom and guidance. Most of the men she'd dated were spoiled pretty boys with more money than brains. They definitely weren't the type of men she would ever marry or turn to for advice.

She had always wanted to apologize to her father for her behavior, but had never had the courage to bring up the subject with him. Since that day, she'd considered their relationship irrevocably damaged. Looking around the bare room, she somehow sensed that her opportunity to tell her father how she felt had passed.

"Miss Smythe?" said the woman, startling her from her moment of retrospection. The woman's voice had a deep timber and held an edge of disapproval. Hanging from her neck by a thin chain was a pair of horn-rimmed glasses. She was wearing a dowdy dress of navy-blue roses over a pale beige background. A button at the neck secured the collar. Her dark hair was shot through with gray streaks and was tied into a bun atop her narrow head.

"Yes. Saffron Smythe, actually."

One pepper-colored eyebrow arched on her pale forehead as she regarded Saffron, obviously unimpressed. "Yes," she said, "Saffron; of course." The woman interlaced her long, tapered fingers on top of the pages of the open book, then leaned slightly forward, her elbows resting on it. Her dispassionate gaze made Saffron uncomfortable. "According to our records, you have arrived slightly earlier than expected."

"Ummmm, that's the thing, Ms ...." Saffron looked at the woman questioningly.

"Ruth. You may call me Ruth." A slight hitch in Ruth's tone suggested to Saffron that she was to continue. Ruth had a small, humorless smile on her lips.

Saffron nodded. "I'm not sure where I am, exactly."

The woman nodded back, unlaced her fingers, and eased back in her chair, her expression signaling to Saffron that she had heard this question many times before. "Of course. Many who arrive here have no idea that their existence on Earth has come to an end."

Saffron froze and her jaw dropped. She shivered as if she was suddenly chilled, except that the room's temperature was nearly ideal. "Do you mean I'm dead?"

A sardonic smile spread across Ruth's features. "Yes. But don't be concerned. You're in the best of hands. I'll soon have your next assignment ready."

"But—I can't be dead," Saffron whispered. "I'm too young. And I'm too rich."

Ruth surprisingly responded with a toothy grin. "I hear that a lot; more often than you might think, actually."

Anger bubbled up from Saffron's stomach. She tasted sour bile at the back of her throat. *How can I be dead and still taste bile?* She sucked in a breath, then exhaled. *I seem to be breathing.* She pinched the skin of her right arm between thumb and forefinger as hard as she could, wincing at the sudden rush of pain. *Son of a bi—*She spat her next words between gritted teeth. "Lady, I don't know who you are, but I'm the daughter of a very powerful man, so I suggest you let me go immediately."

"Oh, but Saffron, no one is holding you here, I assure you. This is a mere way station. My job is to prepare you for your final destination."

Saffron's anger subsided as she eyed the woman. "Final destination?" She had a bad feeling about Ruth's answer. She somehow knew she wouldn't like whatever came next.

A sardonic grin came over Ruth's pale features and her eyes narrowed. "Yes," Ruth said simply, offering no further explanation.

Saffron tried to recall where she had been and what she had been doing before realizing that she was in this windowless room across a desk from this woman who reeked of peppermints. No matter how she tried, it was as if her mind were in a fog.

"It's OK, Saffron. It's unlikely you'll be able to recall anything from the time before you died except for flashes of stray thoughts that may seem like dreams. But don't be concerned. This is often taxing on new arrivals at first, but with time, you will understand. Most find that when they are allowed into the Hall of Memories, they begin to comprehend what they had been in life and what they are now." Ruth spoke as if these cryptic words made perfect sense; Saffron, however, remained thoroughly confused.

This lady is nutso. "OK, I get it, I'm dead and this is heaven … but how did I die?" Saffron froze when an image suddenly formed of herself lying in a bathtub, buried in an ocean of white foam. She was somehow hovering over herself, looking down at her naked form through the dissipating bubbles, lying on her back under the water in the marble tub. Her body was limp, unmoving, her eyes closed. Saffron realized that the 'her' in the bathtub wasn't breathing and that the lips were pale, the skin on her face a sickly gray pallor. A half empty crystal champagne flute sat on the edge of the tub. The bubbles in the wine having long ago dispersed meant that the flute had sat untouched for too long and gone flat.

It dawned on her that she had died while having a bubble bath.

She loved bubble baths, the water lapping against her skin like a silk blanket, the warm steam rising from the white jasmine-scented bubbles. Surely, she wasn't meant to die in a bath? Saffron licked her lips. I loved the taste of champagne on my tongue.

Ruth laughed lightly, causing the corners of her eyes to crinkle. "No, this isn't heaven. As I said before, this is a way station where you will receive your next assignment."

Saffron studied the woman's placid features, then her eyes dropped to look at the book. "What's in the book?" she asked.

"This is a record of each person's date of death. My job is to fill in the column listing each arrival's final destination—once I've been told, of course."

Saffron's eyes narrowed. "Told? Told by whom?"

Suddenly a telephone began to emit a muffled ring. Ruth

smiled and reached down to open a drawer in the desk beside her. She withdrew a telephone as black as licorice, with a heavy black wire trailing off the back of the unit and a dial face on the front, covering a white background depicting large numbers and small block letters under each opening in the dial. There was a receiver in a cradle on the top, attached to the main body by a curled wire. As Ruth set it on the desk with a soft thump, it rang again, only louder, this time since the drawer wasn't muffling it.

Saffron had never seen a telephone like it. Where was Ruth's cell phone?

Ruth picked up the receiver and held it to her ear. "Yes?" She listened intently to whoever had called, her expression changing from pleased, to concerned, to puzzled. Finally, she said goodbye and hung up. Her eyes reflected her astonishment.

She sighed before she spoke. "This happens so rarely I am surprised every time it does." Ruth paused, adding to Saffron's discomfort. Finally, she continued. "I'm advised you are to be sent back to Earth."

She paused again to look into Saffron's eyes, since they must have revealed her excitement.

I'm going home.

"I'm sorry, I'm not being clear. Your spirit will be sent to Earth, but your interaction with living beings will be quite limited." Ruth cleared her throat, Saffron sensing the woman's hesitation. "It appears you have indeed arrived earlier than expected—because you were murdered."

Oh, shit. I'm in trouble! I need Amanda Dark.

SAFFRON HAD no sense of movement, but she suddenly material-ized in Phillip Swann's office, one of many belonging to the law offices of Smythe, Wellington, Goldberg, and Thompson. Her senses were immediately assaulted by the scent of wood polish, which wasn't surprising as the Boston law firm had never removed the original teak paneling, installed when the prestigious firm had opened in 1902. Such expensive wood required constant care to maintain its gleaming, pristine appearance, but the partners were agreed that it added to the firm's elegant image. The firm had represented Boston's social elite worldwide for over a hundred years. Of course, she knew this because her great-great-great-grandfather had been the founder and thus an original partner of the firm. Her father still represented the family name on the masthead.

Before the way station disappeared, as if in a fog, Ruth explained that Saffron had been granted one visit outside the place she was to haunt until the matter of her murder was settled. By 'settled', of course, Ruth meant the murder being solved and the killer being brought to justice. Only then would Saffron return to the way station to be assigned her final destination.

She would be able to interact with one living person as well as experience sensory details of the environment around her since this might help trigger memories essential to solving the crime. Ruth ended by warning her that it might take some time, so she must be patient.

As if looking through a veil of mist, Saffron saw Phillip Swann come into focus. He was seated in a black leather executive chair behind a massive, fifty-year-old teak desk, examining documents from a thick file one by one. The wood of the desk was stained dark and polished to a gleaming shine under the light of the crystal chandelier in the ten-foot-high ceiling overhead. A silver executive telephone was to Phillip's right and a large flat computer screen was to his left. Behind his desk, and running the length of the long office wall, were built-in bookcases containing volumes of law books. One wall was a floor-to-ceiling picture window overlooking the bustling city streets far below. The glass was tinted, so it wasn't too bright in the offices, even on the sunniest of days.

But Saffron's attention was drawn to Amanda Dark, who was seated in a horseshoe-shaped leather chair, watching Phillip from the other side of his massive desk. Amanda was a short woman, just over five feet in height; of medium build, not buxom and not thin; with mouse-brown hair cut to brush her shoulders. Her pleasant features, wide-set curious hazel eyes, and smallish nose meant she couldn't be described as beautiful though she wasn't ugly either. Right now, Amanda's eyes gazed at Phillip with a look in them Saffron knew well. The woman loved the firm's associate more than she was willing to admit.

With his jet-black, curly hair cut military-short, his square jaw, and dimples in both cheeks when he smiled, Saffron well understood Phillip's appeal. His narrow waist and lightly muscled arms under his tailored suits and shirts told her he took care of his appearance, but then, any lawyer whose goal was to become a partner needed every weapon in his arsenal to get there. Phillip Swann was bright, personable, and good looking, so he'd surely make partner someday.

Saffron had met Phillip and Amanda at one of her father's mixers held in the office a couple of times a year. Normally, she avoided such stuffy affairs, preferring to hit the many clubs and bars around Boston with peers her own age; but, for some reason, that day she'd attended the party where she'd met the young, handsome associate and his unlikely wannabe girlfriend.

Amanda claimed to be a paranormal detective. She hadn't explained what the job entailed, but Saffron had soon learned that the plain-speaking woman had helped Phillip on a number of difficult estate cases, resulting in very grateful and very wealthy clients who paid considerable sums to the firm. Once, after a few too many drinks, her father had told her that Amanda Dark was a ghost whisperer and that she could speak to the spirits of the dead. Saffron had thought this nonsense; she didn't believe in ghosts.

But when Ruth asked whom she would like to see on Earth, Saffron had immediately asked for Amanda Dark. Even if she were a fake, she had helped with some big cases for the firm, so she had to have some talent for dealing with the paranormal—either that, or she was the most successful grifter in history. However, Amanda's K-Mart wardrobe of gray cotton slacks, white no-name-brand runners, and sleeveless mint-green rayon top didn't scream flourishing con artist. Saffron doubted the latter was true.

Suddenly, Saffron froze as Amanda visibly stiffened. Amanda was looking right at her, her eyes growing wide—not with fear, but with surprise. She sees me now.

"Uh, Phil, we have a visitor," Amanda said, in a low voice.

"Ummm," said Phillip, his attention focused on a document he was reading from the file folder. "Tell them I'm busy."

"It's not that kind of visitor," explained Amanda, her voice now louder.

Phillip stopped reading as his brow wrinkled, and he looked up at Amanda. "A ghost?" he asked, as if it were an everyday occurrence. In fact, Saffron could have sworn his expression was one of annoyance. "In my office?" He shook his head. "No way. We've never had a ghost in my office. You must be mistaken."

Amanda shook her head, her eyes still locked on Saffron, who stood still with a tight grin on her lips. "In fact, I think it's Robert Smythe's daughter."

Phillip grunted. "Really? Which one?" He scanned the room. "I don't see anyone."

Amanda turned her head to scowl at him as if he were a small child. "Really, Phil, do we have to go through this again?"

Phillip's shoulders relaxed, and he grinned, the dimples in his cheeks deepening. "I'm kidding, Amanda. Surely by now you know when I'm joking?"

The tension in Amanda's body eased and she chuckled. "Sorry, Phil, but you know how I am about my work."

"Amanda," interrupted Saffron, "have you two finished your mating dance yet? I have a big problem I need your help with."

Amanda shifted her attention to Saffron. "Sorry, Ms. Smythe, Phil and I are so used to ghosts and we too often spar verbally in front of them." Saffron's hazel eyes flitted to a grinning Phillip Swann, who eased back in his chair while maintaining his silence, then back to Amanda. "What can I do for you?"

These two seemed to be laughing at her. *I've been murdered, for God's sake.*

A knot of anger formed in her stomach. Old habits from her impetuous, over-privileged youth were going to be tougher to break than she thought. She could not deny it; in life, she had been a rich, spoiled brat, but now that she was dead, she had vowed to be better in the afterlife.

She managed to push the anger away before she spoke. "Please call me Saffron. 'Ms. Smythe' was my late mother, God rest her soul." She paused as the humor faded from Amanda's eyes. Saffron then blurted, "I've been murdered. I desperately need your help to catch the killer."

SAFFRON STOOD on the cold marble floor of the expansive foyer of Smythe Hall, Amanda beside her. The sweeping circular staircase curled up and into the distance to the upper floors of the ten-bedroom, ten-bathroom mansion. The floor-to-ceiling crushed-red-velvet drapes over the tall windows bordering the cool foyer were drawn shut, requiring the large crystal chandelier hanging twenty-five feet above their heads to be lit, even though it was early afternoon on a summer day. The musty air spoke of age and neglect. Saffron realized that something had happened in her family home—something bad.

Amanda coughed to clear her throat. "Phil said your father agreed to meet me ... I mean, us."

"You didn't tell him about me, did you?"

Amanda shook her head. "If I did, do you think he would have agreed to see me?"

Saffron sighed. Of course, Amanda was correct. If she had told Saffron's father that she'd spoken to his dead daughter, he'd have dismissed her as a kook after his money. Her father was a practical man, if nothing else.

"I have a question."

Amanda looked at Saffron with a curious expression.

Saffron continued. "How can I be dead so long but only now become ...." Her words trailed off. She couldn't say the word ghost; it sounded ridiculous.

How long ago did I die? For the first time, it occurred to her to wonder how long she'd been dead.

"When did I die?"

Amanda's brow wrinkled. "Space and time are very different in the afterlife. Time isn't linear—"

She was about to explain more when, somewhere overhead, a generator suddenly whirred to life in the silent, dusty air that stank of stale coffee and burnt toast, interrupting them. Amanda's eyes suggested to Saffron that later might be a better time to talk.

Reluctantly, Saffron agreed. She had a sense that time was short, even though in reality she had more time now than she'd ever had in life.

Saffron saw a slit of light coming from the bottom of a closet door on the left side of the foyer that, as she recalled, had contained her mother's and father's long evening coats.

The slit of light grew brighter as a rumbling sound and the

whine of the generator increased in intensity. Finally, there was a deep thud, and the door of the closet slid aside to reveal a wizened man with white hair in a wheelchair. His gray eyes studied Amanda, his pale brow wrinkled by curiosity.

Saffron sucked in a breath as the man's long fingers worked a control stick on the right armrest of the wheelchair and it rolled out of the closet—now obviously converted to an elevator—onto the marble floor. Tears blurred her vision as she realized that this man was her father.

The once vital, healthy man who drank protein shakes for breakfast, ran marathons, and worked out at the firm's gym three times a week had been replaced by these fossil-like remains.

Amanda's features were lit by a smile as she stepped forward to greet her father in the wheelchair. He appeared worn and tired, his once alert, steady gaze dull and lifeless as if he'd lost hope. His features were gaunt, his cheeks sunken, and his skin had a gray pallor.

Upon fully seeing his appearance, Saffron's heart ached for her father as her eyes welled with tears. Ruth had promised she'd experience everything she saw, heard, and smelled—complete with the accompanying emotional reactions—as if she were still alive, but she'd be unable to offer comfort to those who needed it or speak with anyone other than Amanda.

If I'd only known my father needed me so badly, I would have asked to speak with him instead of Amanda. She may not have been able to solve her murder, but her father needed her, and that was more important right now.

Amanda stuck out a hand, which her father ignored, preferring to keep his hands folded in his lap. He was dressed in a navy-blue tracksuit, his feet covered by slippers that were almost worn through with use. The front of the zippered jacket was covered in soup stains. "Mr. Smythe, it's a pleasure to see you again, sir. How long has it been? Ten years?"

His eyes narrowed. "Do I know you?" he asked, his voice raspy and dry.

Amanda dropped her hand to her side, her smile still bright and inviting. "I'm Amanda Dark. Phillip Swann's friend."

His brow creased in thought for several seconds until he nodded. "Yes, the ghost person. You talk to the dead."

"Yes, sir; I am blessed, or some would say cursed, with that particular gift."

The old man eyed her with one gray eyebrow arched. "My daughter died eight years ago. Are you communicating with her ghost now, is that why you're here?" He snorted bitterly. "And I suppose you want money."

Amanda shook her head. "No, sir; Phillip works for you at the firm and your daughter approached us, asking for our help. We won't be billing anything for my services."

Robert Swann shook his head. "She died in a car accident. Why would she want to talk to me now, after all this time?"

Car accident? thought Saffron. "Amanda, who died in a car accident? I drowned in a bathtub. I remember it."

Amanda nodded to Saffron. "Sir, I thought your daughter drowned."

Robert laughed derisively, his humor tainted with bitterness. "No, no, that was Saffron. That lazy, ungrateful drunk drowned herself after partying all night with her so-called friends. She spent my money recklessly and selfishly. She deserved to die." He paused and hung his head.

"My precious Sadie, she died in the car wreck not a mile from the estate. Her death ended my life's work." A tear escaped his right eye, running down his cheek until it fell off the edge of his bony chin to splash on the foyer floor.

Saffron couldn't believe what she was hearing. If she had been murdered, then either her father had done the deed, or her beloved twin sister had done it. She suspected she'd been drugged, then had passed out in the bathtub and drowned. An engineered accident, covered up by a powerful law firm with friends in high places, including the police department.

"Amanda," Saffron whispered. "Don't go any further. I don't want to know."

Amanda looked at her with wide eyes. "But it means you won't be able to go to your final destination, ever."

"Are you crazy, woman?" asked Robert, his eyes wild and his cheeks flushed by a surge of anger. "Whom are you talking to?"

Amanda turned to face Robert in his wheelchair. "Your daughter Saffron is here with me," she said, glaring at him. "And right now, I must explain a few things to her; then you and I must talk. Sir," she added firmly, her hazel eyes now hard, the smile but a memory.

Robert sagged in his chair, his hands fidgeting erratically in his lap, his face twisted by a scowl.

Amanda faced Saffron. "I checked your file at Phillip's office before I came here." She paused, and Saffron could see the mix of emotions on her wholesome features. The paranormal detective took in a deep breath to steady herself and then continued. "Yes, you died in the bath; drowned, as you say. The police investigated after the coroner determined you had an overdose of sleeping pills in your blood stream.

"The investigation resulted in a ruling of accidental overdose, which led to your drowning. Then there was an entry found in your diary—"

"Sadie wrote the suicide note in Saffron's diary," Robert suddenly blurted, his words angry. "I provided the overdose of pills. I killed my own daughter." He steered the wheelchair across the marble floor, right at Amanda, who stepped aside as he stopped. He stuck out a bony index finger at her. "And I'd do it again. Sadie deserved a chance to run the firm. She was a lawyer, but their late mother, who controlled the real family money, included a clause in her will that required the firm be sold after my death and the proceeds divided equally between the twins.

"Sadie would have saved my firm from extinction. Saffron was a party girl who would have destroyed the firm I built. All she cared about was satisfying her own selfish pleasures. If anything were to happen to Sadie after my death, Saffron would assume control of the firm." He sagged in his chair and his voice dropped to a hoarse whisper. "I couldn't let that happen.

"Sadie would have kept up the family tradition. Saffron deserved to die, so her sister could inherit the business." He paused when his voice cracked. Clearing his throat, Robert shook his head. "It seemed to make sense then .... Now that my own days are numbered, I'm not so sure."

His watery gaze shifted to Amanda. "I realize now I was wrong. Tell Saffron I'm sorry. I made a mistake." He began to sob, and Saffron sensed his terrible pain and regret.

Amanda looked again at Saffron. "Well, what do you want to do?"

Saffron thought for a few seconds and then made up her mind. "I'm going to stay at Smythe Hall by my father's side until he dies. I still love him, and I forgive him."

"You do know you won't be able to change your mind if you decide to stay until your father dies, right?"

Saffron nodded.

The doorbell rang, interrupting them. Amanda went to the window and pulled the drape aside; Phillip stood at the door. She waved to him, then turned back to face Robert Smythe, who gazed back at her with red-rimmed eyes.

"Mr. Smythe, I'm going to leave you now. I wish you well, sir, but I still feel your daughter has made a poor decision. If I had my way, and if there were sufficient evidence, I would go to the police. But I imagine the extensive cover-up of your crime and the fact it occurred ten years ago make any investigation not worthwhile."

Robert Smythe ignored Amanda's words, his eyes reflecting his realization that his murdered daughter's spirit was in the room with them. "What did Saffron decide?"

"She's forgiven you, and will be staying on as the resident ghost of Smythe Hall." The corners of Amanda's mouth curled up slightly as she shared a knowing look with Saffron. "At least for a while."

Amanda then opened the front door and went outside, closing it behind her with a soft thump.

Saffron gazed at her father in his wheelchair, his pale gray eyes fearful, and wondered how long he would live. She would haunt him until then, hopefully helping him to come to grips with what he had done and the consequences he might suffer when his day at the way station came. She wondered where Ruth would assign him. Probably not the place with the wings.

One thing she knew for certain; she would see Amanda Dark again, when the time came.

# ABOUT THE AUTHOR

International selling Star Trek author, Russ Crossley, writes science fiction and fantasy, and mystery/suspense as well as their various subgenres.

His science fiction includes the Blaster Squad stories and many short stories published by various publishers. His upcoming novel is a paranormal adventure featuring the investigator Amanda Dark entitled Dark Territory coming in in early 2020. Most of his titles are available in e-book and paperback editions. Also most of his Blaster Squad titles are also available in audiobook editions.

He has sold several short stories that have appeared in anthologies from various publishers including; WMG Publishing, Pocket Books, 53rd Street Publishing, and St. Martins Press.

He is a member of SF Canada and is past president of the Greater Vancouver Chapter of Romance Writers of America. He is also an alumni of the Oregon Coast Professional Fiction Writers Master Class taught by award winning author/editors, Kristine Katherine Rusch and Dean Wesley Smith.

Feel free to contact him on Facebook, Twitter, or his website http//:www.russcrossley.com. He loves to hear from readers.

# OTHER TITLES BY RUSS CROSSLEY YOU MAY ENJOY

The Trudy Wilson Mystery Novel Series

Bad Loyalty

Shear Murder

Buzzcut - coming soon

Blaster Squad

#1 Terror on the Moon

#2 Sea of Death

#3 Planet of Doom

#4 Raiders of Cloud City

#5 Rise of the Empire

#6 Galaxy of Evil

#7 The Empire Strikes

Mercenary Knights – A Blaster Squad short story

Other Novels

Attack of the Lushites

Revenge of the Lushites

My Zombie Prince

Antique Virgin

The Fire In Their Hearts

with R.S. Meger (from Champagne Books)

Zomopolis

The Last Serial Killer

Razor and Edge Mysteries

The Kidnapping of Billy Buttons

String of Pearls

Death by Clown

Beggin' For Murder

Ragged Ice

The Grand Central Mystery

A Strange Case of Undead Murder

Jazz Stiletto Mysteries

A Day Without Sunshine

Skullduggery

Instrument of justice (first published in Over My Dead Body online
mystery magazine)

The Amanda Dark paranormal mysteries

Hook Island

Grind Manor

Moonrise Diner

A Father's Daughter

Dark Territory – Novel (coming soon)

Short Stories

Countdown

Shoeless Moe

Round Up At The Burger Bar:

The Story of Trixie Pug, Parts 1, 2, 3, 4, 5, 6, 7, 8, 9

Five Minutes

Blossom Queen, Barbarian

The Secret

The Family Line

End of the Flies

Death by Magic

The Penguin Sleeps With The Fishes

Only The Worthy

Hero For A Day

End of Empire

Strange Bedfellows

Big Business

A Perfect Crime

The Wise Guy and The Pirates

In Search of the Perfect Cup

T.I.N. Men

The Legend of G and the Dragonettes

The Incredible Mr. Fix-It

Lock Stock and Barrel

Divided Loyalties

Cave of Wonders

A Family Empire

Until We Meet Again

Dragon Rising

Solitary Man

The Keel Mountain Conspiracy

Angel on My Shoulder

Heroes of Old

The Great Bicycle Race

Tikka's Big Day

"My Partner the Zombie" —
Hungry For Your Love Anthology
(St. Martin's Press)

Big Hairy Deal

One Red Shoe

A Bad Day in Lunden Texas

Bloody Betty, Queen of the Pirates

Mirror Image

Dangerous Waters

Cape Disappointment

Boomerang

The Watcher of Wayburn Street

The Apprentice

Drip!

A Beautiful Friendship and The Parrot of Doom

Robine's Diary

The Christmas Club

Loose Ends

Splatter Pattern

It Takes Two

Lexicon

Replacement Parts

Sidekicks

Lost Stories

Time and Space

Survivors

Neighborhood Watch

Unnatural Immortal

Rum Runner's Lounge

It's A Small Galaxy

A Shattered Man

Betrayed

Replacement Parts

Clubhouse Heroes

Sounds That Angels Make

Muggins Rules – originally published in Fiction River Volume 12, Risk Takers

A Simple Assignment

Captain Virtue and the League of Evil

The Beast of Cadboro Bay


Anthologies

Tales of Urban Fantasy

Five Tales of Bizarre Detectives

Tales of Mystery and Suspense

Tales of Weird Fantasy

Tales of Twisted Crime

Tales of The Unexpected

Tales From Space

10 by Russ Crossley

Round Up At The Burger Bar: The Story of Trixie Pug,

Parts 1- 5 The Beginning

Worlds of Science Fiction and Fantasy

More Tales of Mystery and Suspense

Justice Served

Love Stories

Ladies of the Jolly Roger with Rita Schulz

The Adventures of Razor and Edge:

Five Tales From The Quirky Detective Team

An Unexpected Journey

On Edge

Thrilling Adventures

Total War

Courageous

The Adventures of Amanda Dark

Vagabond 002: Apocalypse Edition

Non-Fiction

The Writers Tools - The Synopsis

The seven books in this galaxy spanning action adventure will thrill space opera fans of all ages.

So strap on your blaster and come along for a ride you will never forget.

9 781927 621721